Forecourt

A note on the author

Katy Hayes was born in 1965. This is her first collection of short stories; the title story "Forecourt" won the Golden Jubilee Award in the Francis MacManus Short Stories Competition on RTE in 1993. She also works as a theatre director. Her first one-act play has been commissioned by the Abbey Theatre. Katy Hayes is married and lives in Dublin.

Forecourt

A collection of Short Stories

Katy Hayes

POOLBEG

Published 1995 by
Poolbeg Press Ltd,
Knocksedan House,
123 Baldoyle Industrial Estate,
Dublin 13, Ireland

A catalogue record for this book is available from the British Library.

ISBN 1 85371 500 X

Cover photography by Mark Nixon
Cover design by Poolbeg Group Services Ltd
Set by Poolbeg Group Services in Garamond 10/12.5
Printed by Cox & Wyman Ltd, Reading, Berks.

The Publishers gratefully acknowledge the support

of

The Arts Council / An Chomhairle Ealaíon.

Acknowledgements

I wish to acknowledge the expert help I received from my editor Kate Cruise O'Brien. The following people have given me guidance and support: Seamus Hosey; Ferdia Mac Anna. I would like to thank my parents Tom and Anna Hayes for their unfailing support. I wish to acknowledge the Francis MacManus Awards and the Mercier Press for giving me their Jubilee prize for "Forecourt". Finally, I would like to thank my husband Tony for his love.

To my sister Trudy
for all the love and encouragement

Contents

Forecourt

I arrive and the garage is sleeping quietly. I have it open and ready for business by six-thirty. I love my job. I got summer holidays on June the sixth, and started work here straight away. I'm only working on the petrol pumps. You have to be here six months before they allow you to start being a mechanic. The manager is a friend of my older sister. She used to go out with him. He is very ugly. My sister's taste in men is fairly dreadful.

I always wear figure-hugging denims to work. They make my bum look nice. I can usually see out of the corner of my eye that all the mechanics are looking at me and my ass. When it's sunny like today, I wear a little vest top with bare arms and a bare neck. I look at my reflection in the mirror. It's a bit clean looking, so I rub a bit of engine oil just over my right breast and on my cheek. It looks really cute. I got a new bra and it makes my boobs look great. It kind of raises them up a bit and points them outwards. Not like the boring yokes my ma gets for me. Sports bras. They're made out

1

of plain white stretchy cotton and they kind of flatten out your tits and tuck half of them under your armpits.

My mother is a feminist. She keeps talking about equality in the workplace, and she says there should be more women in male-dominated jobs. I thought she would be pleased that I had got a job as a petrol pump attendant, but I think she was thinking more in terms of brain surgery. My older sister Pam tells her not to be so bloody bourgeois. When Mary Robinson was up for the presidency my mam made all my brothers vote for her. She said there wouldn't be another hot dinner in our house unless that woman got into the Park. My brothers all joked and said they'd vote according to their conscience. My mother is their conscience. I am too young to vote but I would have voted for Mary Robinson if I could. I think she has great legs. When I'm as old as her I hope I look as good as her. Why can't my mam dress like her instead of wearing denims all the time? She doesn't have the figure for denims. I wish she'd dress her age.

I know all the regular customers. I have great chats with them. There's one man in particular. Colm Cronin is his name. I know 'cos it's written on his credit card. Lovely name. He drives a black BMW. He stares into my eyes as I hand him back his car keys, and winks at me before he drives out of the forecourt. When he asks me how I am, he seems to really want to know.

His missus is also gorgeous. She is like a model. Tall, blonde, lots of suntan. They have one kid, a little girl who is an absolute stunner. Long blonde curls, cute pout. The Missus comes in to me about as often as he does, but during the morning, on her way to do the shopping. She drives a bright red Toyota Starlet. Usually she doesn't pay me, but asks me to put her bill on to his when he comes in later on, and he pays for the lot with his credit card. I'm not really supposed to do that, but so far they haven't let me down. He's always made it in before the end of my shift, so the Boss can't possibly know that I do it.

Sometimes I imagine myself driving the Starlet. I look great in red. I drive home with my kid, I'd call her Saffron, to a beautiful house surrounded by trees, and I'd cook his dinner for him. Something posh out of me mam's Cordon Bleu book. Then he'd come home and fly into a jealous rage and throw the dinner on the floor, on account of him thinking that I'm having an affair with his business partner, but then he'd say he's sorry and couldn't help himself because he's so tormented with adoration for me. Then we'd slip into something more comfortable and lie in each other's arms listening to U2 singing "All I Want is You", then we'd dive into bed and make glorious amazing mega-fabuloid love. No, we wouldn't get as far as the bed. We'd do it on the carpet. We'd devour each other with kisses and bites and eventually we'd do you-know-what, and afterwards we'd lie there panting.

Sometimes I feel a little bit guilty when I see his wife. I wonder has she any idea about me and him.

Though I like my job, it can be a little bit dull. I've figured out a way to keep myself amused. If I position the pump nozzle in such a way while I'm filling the petrol tank, and hold my crotch against the tubing, the vibrations caused by the petrol flowing through make me feel quite excited. It's a lovely tingly feeling. I could do it all day. Especially on a hot day.

As morning becomes midday I am getting hot and sweaty. I spend my time tidying and thinking about what the mechanics would look like with no clothes on. Colm's wife comes in. I fill her up and she smiles at me and tells me that he'll be up later to pay me. When she smiles she is a real smasher, but her eyes are slightly glazed and she doesn't really see me. Most of the customers are like that.

My big sister Pam and her current boyfriend Podge call in to me and try to scab some free petrol. I take off my sister's Ray Bans and hide them under the counter. She'd kill me if she knew I had them. They're real, not fake. She got them in New York. Podge is the ugliest boy in Dublin. He has chronic acne. He is twenty-three and he still has acne! I got a spot once, when I was thirteen. It lasted for two weeks and then it went away. I haven't had one since. Puberty, I suppose. Podge's spots are really angry-looking. I once asked Pam did she close her eyes when she kissed him and she didn't speak to me for two days. He drives a rusty heap of shit. Honestly, it is primitive. Pam, as always, is looking lovely in a gorgeous red and white polka dot mini-dress. There is no point in

Pamela dressing up when she has the Incredible Hulk on her arm. I've tried to tell Pam that it is embarrassing for me that she has gone out with every ugly guy in Dublin. She told me that pretty boys are crap in bed. In my opinion, it isn't a problem if they're ugly in bed, you could switch the lights out, it's just when they're out on the streets in public that they should be presentable. Besides, you spend much longer with them out of bed than in it. Podge pours his own petrol and makes funny faces in the window at Pam, who is laughing loudly. The two of them would have really ugly kids. Pamela coming here annoys me. This is my place. My sister never leaves me alone. No matter what I do she comes along and pokes her nose into it. I'm sick of her.

My kiosk is mostly made of glass so when it is as sunny as it is today it becomes incredibly hot. I try and stand in the shade a good bit, 'cos my shoulders are beginning to burn. The sun is baking down and the air is incredibly still, no breeze at all. I begin to sweat. Colm. Colm. I can't get his face out of my mind. He'll be up later. She said so. Time mooches past in the still heat. He doesn't come. At half past three I begin my end-of-shift routine. I start to count the cans of oil and add up the money. My till is going to be ten pounds short because he hasn't come in to pay for her petrol yet. Never mind, I'll explain to Bob, the three stone overweight boy who takes over from me at four. At a quarter to four, I hear the unmistakeable sound of Colm's engine. I am bent over my figures. As his car comes to a halt I look up and my insides leap. I go out to his car window and he hands me his keys, I see small beads of sweat on his temples and wet patches under his armpits. I can smell him. His eye is caught by the oil smear on my right breast. I colour unnoticeably under the screaming sun, and I feel blood rush to my groin. I open the petrol tank, put the pump nozzle in, and squeeze the trigger. The temptation is irresistible, so I slide my crotch over to it and a shiver goes down my back. I've never done it with his car before. I can feel my breath get faster. He switches on the car stereo and suddenly the air is filled with "All I Want is You". I look at the meter. It reads fifteen ninety five and it's churning fast. The car holds twenty-six pounds usually. The petrol fumes rise to my nose as the sun beats down on the back of my neck and Bono's voice rings out across the forecourt. I pass a point and I cannot stop and suddenly I explode and a noise erupts from inside me, loudly, I hear myself groan, like an animal, as the petrol tank overflows and petrol runs down my jeans, the pump shuts off automatically. I stand there for a moment, the nozzle in my right hand, dripping petrol on the concrete forecourt.

Auto pilot takes over. I hang up the nozzle and walk to the car window. I am terrified of his face. He turns to look at me and his cheeks are as red as his wife's car, his expression astonished. I feel more weird than embarrassed. I feel like my body belongs to someone else. My right breast is still tingling.

I walk into the kiosk with his card and do out his credit slip. He follows me in to sign it. I can smell him really strongly now. He is still staring at me with a bewildered look, though there is a small smile threatening at the corner of his mouth. I look at him, desperate. He puts away his card and goes to give me the usual one pound tip. In mid-gesture he catches my crazy eye and goes scarlet, the colour of his wife's car. He drops the coin and I bend down and he bends down to pick it up. Our heads crash against each other and we both reel backwards, and my head spins. He asks me if I'm all right, the pound coin forgotten on the oily floor. I close my eyes and pretend to faint, and he steadies me. I fall against his chest and he has no choice but to put his arm around me.

There are two other cars on the forecourt, beeping furiously in the afternoon heat but I don't care. I am in his arms. I am in his terrified arms and I don't care.

War

I don't understand why my mammy makes me go
to ballet lessons. I hate ballet lessons. I much
prefer wrestling. I used to go wrestling with boys
from the boys' school in the bottom field during
lunch break, but the teacher stopped me. She said
it wasn't ladylike. She also caught me spitting, and
she said that Our Lady cried every time a girl spits
and I said that I thought Our Lady was in heaven
for eternal happiness and why then would she cry.
Then the teacher asked me how do we clean our
souls, and I said you put a face-cloth down your
throat with soap on it and I was put outside the
door and the headmistress was sent for and I was
told I was the boldest girl in the school and I was
sure I wasn't because I was only in fourth class and
there were much bolder girls in sixth class. I knew
there was. Judith Horgan, who was in sixth class
and lived in Corrig Park and had five skinhead big
brothers, was definitely bolder than me. She went
round the school yard bullying everyone and
telling everyone to f-off.

I quite liked being put outside the door because it meant I didn't have to do lessons. I also liked being sent for to mind my little brothers. One was in baby infants and the other in first class. Peter, the one in first class, had settled now. But Bernard cried for our mammy every day and he only quietened when I came. I liked Bernard better than I liked Peter. I remember when he was born, I was sick of the old baby, and happy to get a new one. The only thing wrong with Bernard was that he wasn't a girl. I really wanted a girl. When my mammy was expecting, I told her that I was praying to God every night for a girl. I haven't prayed to God since. He really let me down on that one.

My favourite colour is red. It used to be pink, but I changed it because my best friend Alison Connolly's favourite colour is red. Alison lives over our back wall. Her garden is the same size as ours, but it is much neater. A man comes every fortnight to do it. We do ours ourselves. Well my mammy does. She likes doing the garden. My daddy likes sitting in it. Alison bites her nails, so I started biting mine too. They taste lovely. Alison and I meet on the wall at the end of the garden and play. She makes me give her all my sweets, but I don't mind. I don't really like sweets. They make me vomit. Alison gets called in earlier than me at night. Mrs Connolly is very nice. Her real name is Harriet Marsh which is what she's called when she's being an actress. She gives us biscuits though she gives out to me about going round in my bare feet. I don't like shoes. My mammy said that she went to school in her bare feet so I thought I should be allowed but Mrs Connolly said that that was in the olden days when people were too poor to wear shoes but I said that I didn't see what good shoes did, except in the winter when it was cold but it wouldn't be winter again for ages because my birthday had just gone by and we were about to get our summer holidays from school so winter wouldn't be until next year.

Our block is called Woodley Grove. Our house has been there a while, but some of the ones around the block are just being built. My mammy and daddy give out about the builder because there is a big waste ground of rubble left which was supposed to be made into a playground but it is full of mounds and ditches and rubbish. Alison and me and Avril Quinn used to play police women and robbers there (Avril Quinn was always the robber) until we were stopped by the older children. It was the Doyle boys who stopped us. They said that we weren't to play there anymore because it was to be their HQ. "HQ for what?" Alison said, and they said for the war against Corrig Park. Corrig Park was the council houses at the next turn on your left as you went down the road towards the old railway line. Some of the girls in my class lived there. They all had more common accents than us, but they were alright. They hated kids from Woodley and we hated kids from Corrig, according to the Doyle lads. Stephen Doyle, the eldest, who was twelve, said that his father who was a policeman said that they were layabouts who were all on the dole and hadn't made any effort to better themselves. After we were talking to them, I asked Alison what was a HQ and she raised her eyes to heaven and said I was pig ignorant. I asked her if we should be so friendly with the girls from Corrig Park in school and she said that she wasn't friendly with them, I was, but this was a lie because just the day before she had asked girls from there to play skipping with her when she wouldn't talk to me at break because I wouldn't share my lunch with her but my mammy had told me not to.

Anyway, we weren't allowed to play on the waste ground anymore which we thought wasn't fair and we were going to tell our mothers when Alison came up with the idea that we could spy on the boys in their war, and maybe they would let us join in. Avril Quinn said she didn't want to play on the waste ground anymore because it was too dirty and her mother always gave out to her when she came home with her white socks dirty so we laughed at her and called her names and told her to go home to her dollies. Then we went to my back garden and started to think up a plan. While we were there we made some mud pies, only we put too much water in them and they wouldn't stick properly. Alison said I should jump off the coal shed with an umbrella as a parachute, since we needed training for war. I did this and the umbrella didn't do much good but I didn't hurt myself anyway because I'm much tougher than Alison because she wears shoes and doesn't climb trees.

Then we had the idea of making camouflage suits, so we started sticking branches and leaves onto our clothes with Sellotape. It was kinda hard to camouflage Alison, 'cos she has white blonde hair and it stuck out a mile. Also her clothes were all bright colours 'cos her mammy likes bright colours. It was easy to disguise me as a bush though. We were just in the middle of all this when my mammy called me in and made me do some reading with my daddy because I was only on Reader 4 and the rest of the class had gone on to Reader 5. I went in and did the reading because Alison had said that she would stop being my friend if I didn't stop being the dunce of the class. But I said that I wasn't the dunce, there were other girls who were far more stupid and were only on Reader 3. But Alison said they weren't dunces, they were retarded and I was nearly retarded. I said that the doctor said that I was dyslexic and Alison said that this was just like being retarded. I told my mother this and she said that I shouldn't play with Alison Connolly because she had bad ideas in her head.

On Saturday we started the espionage. We went out very early and got into position, me disguised as a bush. I stood in line with two other real bushes. Alison said that I looked more like a bush than they did. I was very close to the centre of HQ. The boys met in a tent made out of black plastic bags and sticks. When the boys arrived they went inside and none of them noticed me. Alison was walking the wall over the other side of the waste ground singing *Ave Maria* to distract them from looking at me. One boy, Jamie Kelly, was told to be sentry and he stayed outside and did what he was told because he was only nine. I don't think he was a very good sentry because he just sat in the dust and played with pebbles and didn't even notice that a whole bush had moved right up close to the tent and was listening to the plan. I thought that they wouldn't win a war with Corrig Park if that happened very often. I found out everything we needed to know. The war was going to be Saturday week and the Woodley Grovers were going to go down to Corrig and steal the goalposts from their football pitch and bring the goalposts back here and put them up on the wasteground. After the meeting finished I moved away again, and Alison started to walk the wall and sing *Ave Maria* again. The boys waved at Alison and she waved back. They liked her because she had blonde hair and her mother was sometimes in the newspapers. The boys never waved at me. They said that there was something wrong with me because I liked playing wrestling, and that I wasn't a proper girl.

I made Alison beg me to tell her all the stuff I had learned. To begin with I wouldn't tell her anything but when she got down on her knees and begged and told me I was her very best friend I did tell her. She thought it was great, that I had found out an awful lot. Later on, inside the tent we found a map of Corrig Park drawn in biro on a piece of paper from a copybook. This was our first clue. I got a box at home to put clues in, and kept it under my bed. We played around all the time and noticed that the boys were doing drills and sit-ups to get into training. We got bored doing that, so sometimes we went to my house and played dressing up. Alison sneaked dresses out from her house. We weren't allowed to play in Alison's house because it was too tidy. We were allowed to play in my house though. We were playing dressing up when my little brother Peter the Pest came in and said that he wanted to play with us so we dressed him up too. Normally I didn't like playing with Peter, but it was fun putting a dress and lipstick and high heels on him. My mammy came in and she thought it was very funny and she got my daddy to come and take a look and then they took out the camera and did photographs. Alison loved having her photo taken. She said that she was photogenic like her mother. Later on my mammy said that Alison was a proper little madam. I asked my mother was it true that the people in Corrig Park were all layabouts and more stupid than the people in Woodley. She said no, that was a terrible thing to say. She asked me did I like Cora, our babysitter, and I said yes, and she said that she was from Corrig Park. I said I knew that, and Mrs Connolly had said that she was an unmarried mother and that was why Mr Connolly had to pay so much tax. My mother took the wooden spoon to my legs. I cried for a while, but then I got bored and went to explore the attic.

The Saturday of the war arrived, and me and Alison got up very early. I wore shoes that day because you needed shoes for kicking in a fight. The war was to happen at ten o'clock. The boys were meeting at HQ at half nine. They were all late because they all wanted to watch the end of breakfast telly. Stephen Doyle said that this was no way to win a war. We overheard this and then we ran off down to Corrig Park the back way through the fields and we got to the bit of forest near their green where the goalposts were and we waited. Corrig Park was like Woodley, except the houses were smaller and there was no driveway for cars. The people who had cars parked them on the road. There were two piebald horses grazing on the green. Alison said that this was because the people were knackers.

We waited there for ages. Alison said she was hungry and wanted to go home for some biscuits. I said that we couldn't go home now, or we'd miss it. Soon, the boys arrived, with dustbin lids as shields and sticks. We pretended to be collecting leaves for our nature project and pretended to be surprised to see them. Stephen Doyle said that since we were there, he'd let us hang in with them, though there was a no-girls rule. He smiled at Alison. I think he liked her. She smiled back. Stephen Doyle said that she could be his girl, that he'd wear her ribbon into the battle like they did in the olden days. Alison gave him her ribbon. I was very cross. She was supposed to be my friend. Then, they went away for a while behind a bush and I suspect he gave her a kiss. Alison was always talking about kissing. When they came back, he let

15

Alison sit beside him in the centre of the circle when he was making his plans. I asked Alison to ask could I sit there too but Stephen Doyle said that I had to stand forty paces away from the meeting, so I didn't know what was going on. I only heard the first bit about how it would be so much easier if we had a helicopter.

When they decided to start the war, I rushed forward with them. Alison kept to the back, because Stephen told her to. Some boys had been given the job of digging up the goalposts, other boys were to fight off the Corrig defence. I joined the fighters and I got into a great wrestle with a boy who I recognised from the altar boys. It was a great mill. I managed to give Stephen Doyle a few kicks in the middle of the fight. I don't think he knew it was me. One kick landed right on his shin and I bet it gave him a big bruise. I was fighting away with two Corrig boys when I suddenly realised that the goalposts had been dug up and the Woodley army was retreating, four of them carrying the goalposts back to the little forest and along the back fields. Nobody told me that I was supposed to retreat. Before I knew what was happening, a sack was thrown over my head and my hands were tied behind my back. I heard somebody say that I was a hostage, and they told me to walk. They said they were taking me to HQ and that there would be an emergency meeting with their chief and I would have to answer questions. We walked for ages and ages to get to their HQ but that was because they walked me

around in a circle for half an hour so I wouldn't
know where I was going. That was a bit of a waste
of time, because when we got there I knew exactly
where I was because it was beside the pylon, and
there's only one pylon in the area. When we got
there we had to wait for the chief to arrive. I was
worried because I had told my mammy that I was
going to stay in Alison's for the day and she
wouldn't come looking for me.

They took the sack off me when the chief
arrived. He was taller than Stephen Doyle and he
had a flick-knife. He told me he was going to cut
my eyes out if I didn't give him information. They
tied my hands to a long pole so I was just like
Jesus carrying the cross. I thought they were going
to kill me. I didn't really mind, but I would have
preferred to be a martyr like Daniel in the lions'
den or die for Ireland like Robert Emmet. I didn't
want to die for Woodley Grove. They tied me to a
post and left me there for ages and went for a
meeting to decide what to do. My arms were
getting sore from being stretched out and I wanted
my mother. I was hungry. When they came back, I
told them I was hungry and one of the boys went
off to get food. He brought back lashings of stuff,
Fanta orange, chicken, crisps and biscuits. It was a
great feed. They untied my left hand so I could eat.
They had decided that they would send a note to
the Woodley Grovers asking for the return of the
goalposts in exchange for me. I was worried about
what would happen. They wouldn't think I was
worth a goalpost. Unless Alison put in for me as

her best friend. But I couldn't depend on Alison. She always forgot about me when I wasn't there. Everytime I went on summer holidays, when I came back she was somebody else's best friend. I told them which house was Stephen Doyle's. And off went their messenger with the note. I thought that all the Woodley Grovers had to do was capture the messenger and swap us, but they probably wouldn't think of that.

I asked the Corrig chief if I could have a go on a horse, and he said "No", that I'd only escape. Later on, when he got called in by his mammy to mind his little brothers because she was going shopping, the boy left to guard me let me try out the horse. It was great fun on it. I sat behind the boy and we galloped around the field. I kept saying I was hungry and they kept getting me food. Lovely stuff. I was the best fed hostage ever. Much nicer food than my mammy gave me. The messenger didn't come back for ages and I thought maybe they did capture him, but what had happened was he had to fix a puncture in his bike before he went. He had a note from Stephen Doyle in a sealed envelope addressed to the Corrig chief. We weren't allowed to open it, even though it was all about me. The Corrig chief came back from babysitting and he opened the note. It said that I wasn't a Woodley Grove Army person, I was just a dumb cluck who was doing my nature project in the woods and I didn't count as a POW. They could keep me for all he cared. Signed: Stephen Doyle. Commander in chief. PS. Your goalpost is now firewood. I knew that Alison must have helped write it because she was the only person I knew who said dumb cluck. She always called me a dumb cluck when I was reading in school because I was so slow. So the Corrig Parkers went into a huddle for a meeting and when they came back to me they told me their plan. If I would tell them where our HQ was, they'd let me go after a little bit of torture. I told them, and they tortured me for a while. They made me lie down in the muck, and they made me sing "Woodley Grovers are no good, chop them up for firewood" and they made me kiss the chief's shoes and then they said that the last thing they'd do was to sting my feet with nettles. So I had to take off my shoes and they got a big branch of extra stingy nettles, the boy who got it stung himself terribly, and they rubbed it up and down my feet to make them sting. It was a terrible punishment and I cried very loud. I hated nettles. When I was little I had fallen into a clump of nettles and got stung all over until my daddy rescued me. When I started to cry, they untied me and said I could go. If I'd known that was going to happen I would have started crying much sooner.

It was very sore to walk with my stung feet, but I managed. I went the short way by the road. When I finally got home, my mammy gave out to me about how mucky I was. She said that she was going to take the wooden spoon to my legs again and how was she supposed to keep me clean all the time and it was easily known that I didn't do the washing but I started to cry and told her that my feet were all stung. I didn't tell her about the war or about the Corrig Park boys 'cos she would have got really angry, so I told her I was running in the back fields in my bare feet and I ran into nettles by mistake. She got out some cream and she ran me a bath and put me into my nightie and said I was to go to bed. But I was crying so much that she stayed with me and stroked my forehead and sang me a song. I told her that I wasn't going to be Alison Connolly's best friend any more and she said that she was an empty vessel who made the most noise.

Later that day, I could see it from my bedroom window, hundreds and hundreds of kids from Corrig Park, with their two horses, the chief riding one of them, came up to Woodley Grove. They looked really savage as they walked along to the waste-ground where they found their goalpost. They knocked down the black plastic bag tent and then they went away. I knew that Stephen Doyle would say it was my fault, that I must have told them where HQ was, but what else could I do? Nobody rescued me. Nobody else got stung for torture. Alison called over to me later and I told my mammy to say I was sick in bed. But my mammy didn't answer the door, my daddy did and he didn't know that I wasn't going to be Alison's friend any more and he let her in. She wanted to know all about what it was like being a hostage, and I made her beg me. I made her get down on her knees and beg me, but I still wouldn't tell her. She said if I didn't tell her she wouldn't be my friend anymore, and I said that I didn't care. She went off in a huff.

The next day I called on Laura O'Rourke to see would she come and play in my house. Alison spent the whole day walking on the wall at the end of my garden. I knew she wanted me to come and play with her. Laura O'Rourke was all right, but I didn't have as much of a laugh with her as I had with Alison. Laura wanted to play board games and I hate board games. Laura went home and said she'd come again tomorrow, but I didn't really want her to come. I got out my daddy's binoculars and watched Alison walking on the wall. I liked her best as a best friend. She was the prettiest girl in the class. Everybody liked her. In the binoculars I could see that she was beginning to get a tan. I always went red in the sun, but she always got a tan.

I kept playing with Laura for a week, and Alison kept walking along the wall. Every day. She mustn't have been playing with the Doyles any more. I couldn't stick it any more, so I sent Laura home and I went out to the garden and stood at the bottom of the wall. She took off her favourite bracelet and she handed it down to me and asked me if I wanted it. I did want it. It was a gorgeous red bracelet. I had always wanted it. She hadn't even let me wear it before. She smiled and her dimples were huge. She said that she didn't want to play with the boys anymore because they kept playing football and she had to stand at the side and only watch and cheer when Stephen Doyle did something clever with the ball and she said it was boring. She told me she had done a french kiss with Stephen Doyle and I asked her what was a french kiss and she said I was pig ignorant. When she told me exactly what it was I thought it was disgusting. I didn't want my friend to have done that. It made Alison less pretty to have done that. But she was my best friend. My only best friend. My favourite best friend. So I climbed up on the wall and sat there and we held each other's hands and I looked at my new red bracelet sparkle in the sun.

Stepford

Colette Dorgan lived in a bright sunny home, four bed, detached, three bath, master en suite, manageable garden. Cheshire Downs is the name of the estate. It is on the side of a hill and overlooking a small valley with a stream. Across the valley are more similar houses, but slightly smaller. They are called Cheshire Grove. Colette's house is number seven on a road called Cheshire Avenue. People find it very confusing when they are looking for her house because the next road is called Cheshire Drive, and another is called Cheshire Crescent. When she is having people for dinner she always gives them precise instructions, but they never listen, and are always fifteen minutes late.

Her husband, Martin, is an owner. He calls himself a businessman, but essentially he is an owner. He owns lots of things. A restaurant in town. A string of women's clothes shops. Some offices. Some nightclubs. He makes lots of money. Colette met Martin when she was seventeen. He owned the roller disco she used to go to and they became very friendly. She was a star roller skater, could do swirls and twirls and jumps. You couldn't help noticing her when you went there, she stuck out a mile. He was tremendously taken with her the first time he saw the blur of her spinning on the floor. His only worry was the difference in their ages. He was thirty-seven, she seventeen. They started to date. She was a source of endless delight to him. He was very careful not to take advantage of her, very careful to give her space. He wouldn't sleep with her, despite her virginal demands. He insisted they wait till after they were married. He proposed to her at Christmas, and they were married the following June. During the engagement Colette petered out her visits to the Roller Disco, feeling uncomfortable there, knowing all the regulars talked about her behind her back. She had overheard a group of boys giggling about having seen Martin Dorgan's Missus's knickers when she took a tumble.

Martin Dorgan had bought the house shortly after they became engaged. It seemed ideal. He hired a firm of interior designers to do it up, and they had done a lovely job. When he and Colette returned from their honeymoon, he carried her dramatically across the threshold and into the house. She was astounded by the beauty and luxury of the place. She was an only child, had been reared carefully and guardedly by her widowed mother in circumstances close to poverty and her sheer joy in Martin's arms made her think that life had become one of the fairytales her mother used to read to send her to sleep. Martin took her by the hand and led her around the house, and each room was more beautiful than the one before. The front room was first. It was as big as an acre, and the green carpet reminded her of a golf-course. The dining table was made of Waterford Crystal and the drapes were made of pure gold, lined with crushed velvet. Behind the curtains were french doors which led out on to a balcony patio with a barbecue. Colette squealed with delight. She loved patios. The kitchen was like the interior of a cockpit, all knobs and shiny lights and a low flying air vent. Later Colette would amuse herself by turning off the overhead lights and looking at the lights of the appliances. It was full of liquidisers and food processors and blenders and weighing scales. The surfaces were black marble and the machines were charcoal grey. Off the kitchen was her room, where she was to bring her friends for "cosy chats", he said. Her friends were all filling in forms for the bank and the civil service. She wasn't sure how well they'd fit into her house. He had never been too keen on their company. She had to agree with him that they were a little bit childish. They giggled about boys all the time. But that was their job. They were seventeen-year-olds, after all. It was a lovely room, with an open fire and sofas and a dressing-table with drawers. The dressing table was made of walnut, she would learn later, when she did a night course in antiques to broaden her mind. The next room was his study. It was small, with a great brown desk full of little drawers and cubbyholes and a smell of leather. There were filing cabinets and towering bookshelves that reached all the way up to the ceiling, and three telephones.

Upstairs, the rooms were equally astounding. Firstly there was a baby's room, with a cot and mobiles of chimpanzees hanging from the ceiling. Then there was a larger room painted in yellows with one single bed, and an even larger one painted in warm browns with two single beds. The landing was huge, with a stained glass skylight. She looked around at the three open doors of her future children's empty bedrooms. "Fill us," they seemed to say. "Fill me with a baby," the little room said. "I'd like a teenager," said the yellow room. "I'd like boy twins," said the brown room. As she was thinking this he put his hand on the mound of her tummy and whispered into her ear "And you have an empty room which I would like to fill."

Unexplained desires engulfed her. Babies. She wanted lots of them, so they would keep each other company. She wanted hundreds of them. She wanted to be pregnant every year.

"I've left our room till last," he said and he opened the last remaining door. It was huge. Monstrous. The bed was as big as a boat, and the carpet was a two inch pile of blue seas. She was speechless. He opened the built-in wardrobe and showed her its contents. It had a rack of eight dresses which he had bought for her. Then he took her into the bathroom which was off the big bedroom. It was truly palatial, a sunken, enormous bath, shell shaped fittings, a huge mirror.

Martin had engaged an army to come and look after the house. The gardeners came on a Friday. Mrs Curran came every second day to clean up. Jason a handy man came occasionally, but everything worked, so he rarely had anything to do except the windows. Mrs Curran reminded Colette of her mother. She always felt bad when she came, and tidied the house to "get it ready" for her. Colette wasn't used to being picked up after. Mrs Curran always asked for instructions, but Colette could never think of anything, so Mrs Curran just improvised. She had four children, and a house of her own to take care of. When she was in the house, Colette always hid in the bedroom, pretending she was busy with her letters, full of shame. Later, when the babies arrived, and Martin's dinner parties became more frequent, Colette depended on her more.

Colette brought only one item from her old life into her new one. Her roller skates. Her mother had bought them for her on her fifteenth birthday, and they were a magnificent expensive pair, covered in silver spangles. The day after they returned from their honeymoon, after Martin had gone out to work, and Mrs Curran had said her polite good-byes, Colette put on the skates and tried out the patio. It was excellent. For the first few months, this was how she spent most of her days, twirling and swirling on the patio. It was fine for a while, but the confines of the patio soon began to annoy her and occasionally, she went to the park, where there was a wide flat space where local children played on their skateboards. Here she could get up some real steam. Each day she walked to the local shop, a Spar shop, to buy milk and the newspaper. He liked the paper to be there when he came home. She passed other women sometimes, who smiled and said "Hello Mrs Dorgan." And she smiled back. She didn't really feel like "Mrs Dorgan". The title always made her start. She felt different from the other women. Firstly, she was much younger; secondly, her accent wasn't as grand as theirs. She wondered did Martin mind that her accent wasn't grand. She asked him.

"I think your accent is wonderful. I think you are wonderful, and part of you is your accent. I wouldn't swap you for a hundred fancy accents. What are you talking about?"

"Nothing, I just wondered. I don't feel that I fit in with your friends, or the women around here. I think that they all look down their noses at me. They think that I'm a gold-digger."

"A gold-digger?"

"I overheard the woman from the end house in the Spar yesterday. She said I was a 'counter-jumping gold-digger'."

"Well, if that's how broad her mind is, all she deserves is your pity, my darling."

After a couple of months in Cheshire Downs, Colette began to feel less awkward but only inside

28

the house. She still didn't like going out, and she never opened the front curtains. She asked the gardener to plant a high hedge of laurel bushes around the front so nobody could see in and this made her feel better. But she still wasn't entirely happy. She decided to ask some of her old school friends over for dinner. She invited Janet, Statia, and Marge. Janet had got a job in the bank, Statia and Marge in Roches Stores as shop assistants. Dinner went fine, the girls were intimidated by Martin to begin with, and said nothing, but they glugged back their wine fast enough, and in time they became more boisterous. They started to talk about boys. Colette sensed that Martin was bored by the chatter. She wasn't surprised when he excused himself immediately after dessert and went to his study, saying they could all have a good girly chat. The chat didn't work for Colette anymore. She had lost interest in their concerns, and they had no interest in hers. Marge drank too much wine, and became quickly stocious. Eventually she had to go to the bathroom to vomit. Statia wasn't much better. Finally, it was with a sigh of relief that Colette phoned them a taxi at midnight. After they giggled and gurgled out the door, Martin emerged from his study.

"What awful girls," he commented.

"They're my friends," Colette said defensively. "It isn't surprising that you don't fit in with them, since I don't fit in with your friends." But in her mind, Colette agreed with him. They were awful. They had no idea how to behave. Their speech was common. Their horizons low. She wouldn't ask them again.

A few weeks later, Colette bought a home pregnancy testing kit at the local chemist.

"Best of luck with that, Mrs Dorgan," the chemist greased at her as he handed her her change. Colette hadn't realised that the chemist knew her name.

"It's not for me, it's for a friend," said Colette, suddenly self-conscious, suddenly feeling like she was caught doing something she shouldn't be doing. She went home and did the test, and it turned out positive. She had missed two periods, so she reckoned she must be about eight weeks gone. She supposed it was inevitable. If you have sex often enough, you will eventually become pregnant. She was happy about it, kind of. Immediately she phoned her mother. Her mother was delighted. She waited until dinner to tell Martin. When he arrived home, she was all dressed up, and he sensed that something was up. He was delighted with the news, and they went out to celebrate. When he put his arms tightly around her, she knew that she was loved, totally, utterly and truly.

It was a few weeks after that that Colette had her little accident. She was skating, doing twirls and swirls in the back patio and her back went. She fell to the ground in complete agony and could not move. She lay there for hours, until Martin came home from work. She was unconscious when he found her and immediately phoned an ambulance. It turned out to be reasonably straightforward, a slipped disc, very common in early pregnancy, the doctors told her. It really wasn't the wisest, to be doing complicated exhibition rollerskating when pregnant. Really, she had better stop. Martin was furious with her.

"Haven't you any sense? I assumed you'd stop skating and take a bit of care of yourself. You could have killed yourself. What if I hadn't come home so early from work?"

Colette told everybody she was sorry. She hadn't realised that her body would change so early on. She had only been doing some very straightforward twists and spins. Nothing dangerous. Nothing difficult. Nothing she couldn't do in her sleep. She hung up her skates and had to stay in bed for four days. Her mother came and looked after her. While she lay in bed she got to thinking. Something wasn't quite right. She had no needs or wants. She loved Martin, and he loved her, she was delighted to be pregnant. She couldn't figure out what was wrong, but she was unhappy. Maybe it was because she had no friends. She was lonely and miserable. Even her mother couldn't cheer her up. She stayed in bed for four more days. Martin was now sleeping in the other room, because his tossing and turning upset her in the night. Finally, after ten days, she got up and began to tune in to the growing life inside her belly, and a quiet cheer entered her soul, warming up the chill that had taken root there.

She went shopping. Martin had given her a credit card. It read Mrs Colette Dorgan, but she had never used it. Shopping turned out to be excellent fun. She bought hundreds of things. Lots of big dresses that she could be comfortably pregnant in. And some smaller ones, for when she got her figure back. She bought a different style of dress, two-piece suits and John Rocha pants, just like the other women on the estate wore and threw out her old girly jeans and ra-ra skirts. She got new wheels for her skates with extra ball bearings in them. She took up an antique restoration class and a cookery class. She threw out the furniture she didn't like, and went to auctions and bought antiques which she worked on herself. Martin was very impressed with her handiwork, and wondered might she make a business of it. She cooked fancy meals. She polished her skates, and pledged that the first thing she was going to do once she was on her feet again after the birth was go skating in the park.

The baby came, a beautiful bouncing girl. Martina they called her, for her father. Colette could not explain her joy after the birth. Such a beautiful little bundle. Such a tiny little delicate thing. Martina occupied all her time. She loved to bundle her up and take her out. The women in the Spar shop seemed to like her now. They goo gooed over her, and offered to lend her things for the baby, warned her about teething and nappy rash. She wore her hair up, out of the baby's way. Martin came home every day with a new gadget for Martina. Little harnesses and high chairs and bionic rattlers. Colette was happy once again, and only

32

occasionally noticed her skates hanging under the stairs gathering dust.

When Martina was four months old and weaned, Colette began to sneak out at night, when baby and hubby were asleep, and slip over to the park with her skates. People driving home late at night from cocktail parties to Cheshire Downs would see her, a little slip of a figure on skates dancing along the roads towards the park in the moonlight. They thought she must be a local teenager, her hair flowing in the light, her jeans closely hugging her tiny figure. Martin and baby never noticed she was gone. He slept like a log, and Baby like a little log.

Colette became hyper-efficient in the home. She enjoyed all her gadgets. She chopped vegetables and zapped them in the microwave. She loved the sound of the "ping". Her food processor was her best friend. She talked to it all day. That was when she wasn't talking to the baby. She talked baby language to the baby, but addressed the food processor as though it were an adult. She talked baby language to Martin too. She spoke to him with a slight lisp. She thought he liked it. In fact, she was wrong. Martin worked very long hours. He was what is commonly termed a workaholic. He was always at his desk by seven-thirty in the morning, and rarely home before eight at night. Consequently he didn't see as much of his wife as he would like to, but he saw enough of her to realise that the lisping voice she put on for him irritated him hugely. It served to remind him that she was twenty years his junior, a fact that he was striving to forget. Occasionally he asked her to stop, and she did stop for a while, but always slipped back into it.

She got really into her washing-machine. It had an extraordinary collection of cycles. All sorts of spins and rinses and temperatures. Some good for silks, others good for woollies. She tried out lots of different brands of fabric softener and ordered manure for the laurel bush hedge to make it grow really tall. In the summer she mowed the lawn twice a week. She didn't like the grass growing and sprouting daisies, it looked untidy. She kept it as bald as Sinead O'Connor's head.

Two more bald heads arrived. Little twins. A boy and a girl. She called the boy Ken, after her best friend the Kenwood Chef and the girl Lenora, after her favourite fabric softener. She told Martin that the names were out of her special fairytale book that she had when she was a kid. Martin asked the gardeners to build a light fence to obscure the washing line from the view of the living-room window. He didn't like the visitors looking at their underwear, he said, and the washing line was always full. Colette kept washing the clothes, even though they were barely worn. She herself changed about three times a day. In the morning she wore something comfortable, for working around the house; in the afternoon, she changed into a light suit, more formal and outdoory; and she always dressed up for dinner. Frequently she sent clean clothes to the drycleaners because she thought they needed freshening up a little. She loved sitting at the patio doors and looking out at the garments and sheets flapping in the breeze. It gave her great joy. She thought Martin's new anti-washing camouflage fence spoiled the garden, and only became reconciled to it when the sweet peas that the gardeners planted in front of it bloomed. In the front garden, the laurel hedge had grown so tall that it completely obscured the house from the road. Colette finally relented and began opening the curtains at the front of the house. She instructed the gardeners to keep the hedge tightly pruned, now that it was high enough. She loved the look of the hedge with its tight straight lines, you could draw a margin with the edge of it.

The twins were even more dotey than Martina had been. Colette got a double buggy with four wheel drive and an automatic brake. It was a bit difficult to negotiate down the aisles of the Spar, but she managed heroically. She used to park it on hills all the time, because the brakes were so good. She went shopping less now, because the three tots were difficult to manage all together. This upset her, so for her twenty-first birthday Martin got a special harness made so that she could carry Martina on her back and the tiny twins in front. It was specially constructed by a firm in England which made steadicams for the movie industry. It balanced the babies perfectly on her upper torso, but redistributed their weight so that it was absorbed by her hips. Martin had done the original design, and told her that this was the secret of a woman's body. A woman's strength is located in her hips, not her shoulders. She could carry the whole world, so long as she did it with her hips. Martin commissioned a market research study to see if there would be a demand for this product. He was never one to miss a trick. When Colette went out with her harness of babies, the kids she passed on the road called her "SuperMom". She liked that.

Once again, when the babies were weaned, she started to slip out at night and go skating. She was no longer alone when she did it. Some of the Cheshire children were old enough now to sneak out at night. There were two fifteen-year-old girls from Cheshire Grove, a sixteen-year-old boy from Cheshire Avenue and a fifteen-year-old boy from another estate across the main road who frequently came to the park to experiment with group sex. They groped quietly in the corners behind bushes, and Colette paid them no heed as she skated merrily and happily along the paths. The first night she had met them there, they were terrified. The Cheshire boy came up to her and begged her not to tell their parents they were out. She told them she wouldn't as long as they didn't tell her husband. A cameraderie developed between the teenagers and herself. She would occasionally sit with them on a park bench and smoke cigarettes, drink their cider, tell them about contraception and give the boys precise instructions on how to find the girls' clitorises. They all loved Mrs Dorgan. She seemed to understand them in a way that their own parents didn't. They got their daddies to buy them rollerskates, and Colette taught them how to skate. She thought they had the makings of a fine formation team. They brought a ghetto-blaster to the park, and practised to hip-hop music. They lost interest in the group sex thing and flung themselves into treble spins and loop the loops with great enthusiasm. Soon, all the kids in Cheshire Downs were rollerskating. Up and down the roads, from the age of seven, children of all ages were zooming about. A rollerskating plague had descended. Shoppers took their life in their hands going into the Spar, constantly in danger of being rammed by a kamikaze kid on skates. The midnight gatherings in the park were a closely kept secret, though. Only the select few were initiated. The general principles of formation skating filtered down to the other kids on back garden patios in the afternoons. It couldn't be kept a secret forever though, and one of the boys made a new best friend in school who was a bit of a blabbermouth, and soon more and more kids were turning up at midnight on the Friday and Saturday nights.

Cheshire Downs parents couldn't understand why their kids slept so late at the weekends. Probably worn out from all that demanding school during the week. As time went on, Colette hired ballet videos from which to get choreography ideas and brought classical music tapes to the midnight sessions. Martin was delighted by her newfound interest in classical dance. It made her seem more cultured. She was soon an expert on both English and Russian ballet, and he would frequently bring the topic up at dinner parties purely for the pleasure of listening to her chattering on the subject.

It had to happen and eventually it did. Mr Johnson followed his son out the back door one night to the park. When he got to the open concrete space, he was gob-smacked. He had expected to find his son sitting around a bonfire drinking cider, which he believed young people did nowadays. There in the moonlight, were forty or fifty kids doing an intricate formation dance to music from *Swan Lake* emanating from a ghetto-blaster. He sat breathless in the bushes, and watched as the lead swan came on and did a most stunning series of intricate leaps and spins. He didn't recognise her, but she seemed a little older than the rest of the kids. Perhaps about eighteen. He didn't disturb them, he watched for an hour, and eventually, as it looked as if they were breaking up, he sneaked off home before them and left the back door on the latch for his son.

During the week, Colette busied herself with her home and her babies. She was beginning to settle in nicely now. Martin could tell she was content. He came home each evening to a sparkly wife and three sparkly children. She dressed the children for dinner too. She had got some formal wear baby-gro's in Brown Thomas, which she thought were totally cute. They were made out of black and white towelling with a little white ruffle down the front and a dicky bow. She let Mrs Curran do almost all of the tidying now, as she didn't have time, and couldn't believe that she used to hide when she came. Ken and Lenora thrived. Martina went off to playschool. She still talked to Kenwood the food processor. She still lisped at Martin. She still laughed when the microwave went "ping". She still wore her SuperMom harness.

Mr Johnson told Mrs Johnson about the extraordinary sight that greeted him when he followed young Frederick out; Mrs Johnson told Mrs Carraher when they were at the hairdressers and Mr Carraher told the Jenkinses while they were playing golf. The Johnsons and the Carrahers and the Jenkinses met for dinner in the Johnsons' house to discuss the problem. They talked about it over dessert, in hushed tones so as not to be overheard by their kids who were playing music in the next room.

The outcome of the meeting was that the following Friday a band of parents sneaked out into the moonlight fifteen minutes after their children, drove the long way round to the park and climbed over a wall and along a path through the heavy shrubbery to approach the amphitheatre from the opposite side. They were all dressed up in woollies and wellies. Mr Johnson had plotted a route in a recce the preceding Thursday. They settled themselves in a bush, and waited. In little groups of twos and threes the kids arrived. Mr Carraher had brought his Super 8 high density video camera (a present from his wife the previous Christmas) and he lay down in the muck to get a good angle for videoing the proceedings. Mrs Jenkins found a good tree to climb up in order to get a better view. She was joined on her branch by Mrs Carraher. Mr Johnson and Mr Carraher settled themselves with their ornithology glasses in a big bush where they kept laughing and having to shush each other. Finally, when there were about fifty kids assembled, they started. The overture sounded, and once it crashed to a close, the figures danced, disciplined, graceful, beautiful. A tear came to Mrs Carraher's eye as she watched her clumsy pre-pubescent daughter, Carmella, execute a complex series of movements around the other kids. Carmella was a disappointment to her mother. She was fat and ungainly. Her mother hoped that at least she might become intelligent, but alas, this didn't seem to be happening. She did have an interest in cooking though, so perhaps her future lay in that direction. This night, for the first time ever, Mrs Carraher thought Carmella beautiful, as she flipped and spun around the other kids. She sniffed quietly to herself on her branch of the tree. Soon the chief swan appeared, followed by bearers carrying torches looking like fireflies. The parents weren't so keen on this. It looked a little dangerous. Mrs Jenkins had noticed that her paraffin stove wasn't lasting as long as it used to. They each strained their eyes to see if they could recognise the chief swan, but none of them could. Mr Carraher said that he'd look at the close shots on the video tomorrow and see if they could figure it out.

The next day they did figure it out. It was Mrs Carraher who recognised Mrs Dorgan. Mr Carraher didn't believe her.

"Mrs Dorgan, the woman in the frumpy suits with the harness of babies?"

"Yes that's her. You see, you don't remember when she first came here, before she had the babies. That's what she looked like. Denim jeans, flowing hair. Slip of a thing. She looked as if she was fourteeen or fifteen, though they tell me she was eighteen when they married. What do you think of that? An eighteen-year-old girl getting married to a thirty-eight-year-old man. It's a bit queer, isn't it? No wonder she's out doing queer things in the middle of the night. What should we do?"

They decided to consult the parish priest on the matter. Mr Carraher was quite friendly with him on account of them both serving on the local school board. Father Devlin watched the video carefully, looking out for any signs of devil worshipping, which was what he imagined the whole thing to be about. He couldn't see any definite signs, but he was suspicious, especially about the firefly part. They looked distinctly hellish. If it was all so innocent, why did it have to be done at dead of night under cover of darkness? If it was only a roller-skating ballet lesson, what was wrong with the school hall on a Saturday afternoon? Father Devlin had always been a bit suspicious of Mrs Dorgan. He felt there was something odd about her, the way she carried all her babies around the neighbourhood in that strap thing. Flaunting her fertility, as if she had created it herself, rather than received it as a gift from God. He resolved to go and visit her husband.

Martin was more than a little surprised when he opened the door to Father Devlin one day when Colette was out shopping. He wondered did he want more contributions to the school, but Father Devlin seemed to want a chat. He politely asked did he have a video machine, and politely asked if he could put something on. Martin thought this was odd. Perhaps a video of some charitable activities. He presumed Father Devlin was looking for money, and would have been happier to just hand it to him rather than have his time wasted watching videos. Puzzled, he looked at the video, a badly shot account of a night-time roller-skating dance, with formation movements and fireflies. He recognised the ballet, it was like one of the ones that Colette watched. The video zoomed in for some close shots, and suddenly there she was, that lost expression on her face as she twisted and turned, as though nothing else in the world existed apart from herself and the dance. There she was, the girl he had fallen in love with, who had been replaced by the semi-automaton who kept his house, shared his bed and lisped at him. He wanted to climb into the video and embrace her. Her little body, which normally looked so frail, stormed and twirled like that of a finely tuned athlete. Martin had always thought Colette delicate, but here she was like a tiger. Now you could easily see how that slim little body had spat three huge babies into the world.

"When and where was this shot?"

"Last Saturday at 2am in the park."

"By whom?"

"Mr Carraher from Cheshire Grove. The bad fairy in the video is his daughter, Carmella Carraher. Am I to understand by your reaction that you had no idea that this was going on?"

"Yes." Martin suddenly realised that here was a whole part of his wife's life that he knew nothing about.

"Well, it has to stop. Obviously."

"Why?" said Martin. As he'd watched the video he had an overwhelming desire to learn how to skate. He wanted to be able to skate and to play the prince.

"Because it's bad for the children to be up all night, not to mention the disobedience and disrespect shown to their parents. And it shouldn't be seen to be condoned by an adult, like your wife. Now, either you get your wife to stop, or I tell all the other parents, and they'll lock up their children at night."

That was the end of the midnight dances.

Colette obediently opened a roller-skating class in the school on Saturday afternoons. To begin with, most of the night-time crew came, but they soon got bored. It wasn't so much fun during the day, with their parents watching from the tea gallery. They also weren't allowed to do the fireflies. Mrs Dorgan was different. She didn't talk to them as much. They couldn't smoke fags on their breaks, nor could they have a can of cider after the rehearsal. They stopped coming, and after a short break, they resumed their sneaking out at night and went back to groping each other in the bushes of the park.

As the numbers dwindled in the Saturday afternoon classes, Colette's heart went out of the skating. Her favourites of the kids didn't come anymore. Her favourites were the bold ones, the ones who didn't like doing what they were told, and they were the first to disappear. Martin was very sweet to her about it all. He hadn't been cross about the midnight sessions, just sorry they were put a stop to before he could have seen one. One Saturday afternoon, the class was stopped forever by Colette doing a spin, and collapsing to the ground in agony. Her disc slipped again. The same one. She guessed rightly that she was pregnant again and hung up her skates once more.

This pregnancy wasn't as joyful as the other two had been. She just couldn't settle into it. Her bad back meant she couldn't use her SuperMom harness, so she was housebound. She still talked to Kenwood the food processor and she still laughed when the microwave went "ping". She put back on her maternity dresses. Martin became busier and busier, so he stayed out later and later each day. One of his businesses was in crisis, and he was fighting to save it. Colette really felt for him. He couldn't bear the idea of failure. Mrs Curran continued to come, and Colette became fonder of her. The two women chatted and had coffees together. The scandal of the midnight sessions had spread, and reached Mrs Curran. She told Colette that she had heard that there was devil worshipping and group sex orgies. Colette laughed this off, but it did hurt her. The local kids had stopped being friendly to her. They looked suspiciously at her as she walked to the Spar. Their parents had told them that she was a queer one, that a normal person wouldn't be sneaking out at night unbeknownst to her husband.

Colette got more manure for the laurel hedge, which had grown to about fourteen feet by now. She still got the gardeners to trim it to a hard edge. She seemed to have more energy than she could offload these days. Her pregnancy kept her relatively immobile, but it didn't use up her energy. She took up knitting. Ferociously, she knitted. Hats, scarves, cardigans, bed-socks. The baby arrived, a little boy, and she put him into the spare room. It was the last room. She had filled all of them, as she had thought she would on the first day she had come to the house in Cheshire Downs.

When the new baby was weaned, she thought about resuming her nightly flits on the skates, but decided against it. People would be on the look-out for her, she would have no privacy. Instead, she stayed in and cuddled up to the sleeping Martin. It was at this time that the nightmares began. At first, they were quite straightforward. She would dream that she had clothes-pegs attached to her nipples and that her body was tied from head to foot in her own washing line. She would ask Martin did he do it, and he would say "No, you must have been sleepwalking." In terror, she would wake up, and there would be no ropes and no clothes-pegs, and Martin would be snoring gently by her side. Later on it became uglier. She dreamt that she was trapped inside a microwave, and was being cooked alive. She could clearly feel the microwaves pass through her. Out the glass door she could see Martin making himself a cup of tea and she was calling to him, but he couldn't hear. Finally, the machine went "ping" and Martin opened the door and let her out and she screamed at him why had he put her in it and he said that he hadn't, that she had climbed in there herself, and set it to automatic timer. And then she woke up in terror and there was no microwave, just Martin sleeping quietly by her side. The worst dream was that Kenwood, the food processor, had its liquidiser attachment fitted to it and was fucking her. It was plugged into the socket in her bedroom where she normally plugged in her hairdryer and it was energetically fucking her. When she woke up she could clearly feel the instrument's hugeness sitting in her cunt, but when she put her hand down to feel it, there was nothing there. Martin dozed peacefully by her side.

What finally made her decide to move house was the hedge. She woke up one morning and opened the curtains at the front of the house. Her beautiful laurel hedge had been levelled. It looked as though several bodies had jumped up and down on it. Its splendid straight lines had been turned into bellies and contours. Its majestic fourteen feet had been reduced to four. When she went out to inspect the damage, there were cider cans strewn about. It had been the local young people. Colette had thought that her friendship with the kids would have immunised her against these random acts of suburban petty vandalism. Other women on the estate had spoken about midnight raids on their washing lines, and ritual beheadings of tulips, but nothing had ever happened to Colette's house. Until this. Frankly, she wouldn't have minded the tulips, or the washing line, but her hedge, which she had grown herself, which she had loved and nurtured, she needed as her shade against the world. The flattened hedge brought forth torrents of tears. Little Martina toddled by her side and gave her a hug of comfort, but the tears just flowed, out her eyes and down her cheeks and onto the green golf-course floor of the front room.

Politico

Jeananne became a feminist when she turned eighteen. She went to UCD and met a fabulous lecturer who inspired her. Dr Oestes was a very beautiful authoritative woman who lectured in critical theory, a subject which drove Jeananne wild with excitement. Jeananne developed a sort of crush on Dr Oestes and wangled her way into her tutorial each year, where she became the star student. But she had a rival, Cormac.

From the first day that he walked into the class, he was her enemy. That very first day. They had been looking at one of Sylvia Plath's poems and Jeananne had rubbished it, saying that it was a typical whining defeated female voice. She exaggerated her views slightly for effect. Cormac had almost dived from his seat to throttle her in Sylvia Plath's defence. He seemed more than irate at the insult to the dead writer. Jeananne was appalled at his outburst, and thereafter dubbed him the "fanatical literary critic". Dr Oestes seemed to be somewhat impressed by his passion.

When their first term major essay results were

due out, Jeananne went discreetly to the board every day to check. She didn't care where she came on the list, so long as she beat Cormac. When the list finally went up with her name at the top of it, she smiled coolly across the concourse at him, her smile loaded with malicious pride.

"Hi," he called back, taking her smile for a greeting. They never spoke out of class.

Dr Oestes started a women's group, and Jeananne was the first to sign up. The group functioned quite well as a forum for personal and political discussion and as a general focussing aid on feminism. Cormac headed a deputation from a number of men who wanted to join the women's group. After democratic discussion amongst the group it was decided that certain sessions would admit men, and others would exclude them. At Cormac's first meeting, he made a beautiful speech about how honoured he was to have been admitted to this sanctum. It was like gaining access to the womb. He felt that if men and women worked together towards an egalitarian society, nothing would stop the tide of feminism. He was an impassioned and highly skilled speaker, the burden of strongly held unpopular beliefs through his adolescence having sharpened his tongue. This particular speech was more reserved and humble than normal, same cunning fox though, just a slightly different register. The other women all swallowed him. Jeananne didn't.

Not only did they tangle in class, they now started to spark off one another in the women's group. He would preface all his arguments with a humble acknowledgement of the inferiority of his views, owing to his not possessing ovaries, and then go on to contradict her on everything. You would scarcely believe that they both claimed to represent the same political creed. One day he annoyed her so much that she wanted to thump him. She started to completely ignore him on the campus and in the restaurant. The only intercourse between them was in class or in the women's group, where they sparred in clipped post-structuralist language. Jeananne hated him, but she came to look on him as a stone upon which to sharpen her developing intellectual powers. The others in the women's group couldn't understand Jeananne's antipathy to this boy. After all, male feminists weren't tuppence ha'penny. Those that existed should be cherished, or at least encouraged. They felt that Jeananne was being unreasonable about him.

One day, when she was drinking coffee in the restaurant, he came over to her and asked if he could join her.

"It's a free restaurant," she went back to her newspaper. Cormac gathered his courage and gently took the folded newspaper from her hand. Jeananne, outraged, snatched it back.

"Look, Jeananne, I know you don't like me and I'd really like to know why. What have I done? You and I should get on great together, we think broadly alike on so many issues, though we always end up fighting like dogs over the detail. I would really like to be your friend."

Jeananne stared at him, and then picked up her newspaper and her coffee and moved to another table close by. She watched him out of the corner of her eye as he slowly buried his head in his hands on the table. She wasn't sure why she disliked him so much, but suspected that it was his ego that bothered her. That, and the fact that they had the same interests. She'd always been fiercely competitive.

From then on their relationship just levelled off into a plain and fairly ordinary dislike. They were both elected to the organising committee for the campaign for abortion information for women, so they had to do quite a lot of demanding work together. Each learned the value of restraint and compromise.

The women's group organised a "reclaim the night" march to celebrate International Women's Day. Cormac and Jeananne again worked side by side on the organising committee. Cormac was not allowed to attend the march though, because it was women only. He argued this point heatedly with Jeananne and others. He felt it was separatist that he wasn't allowed to go, that the march would defeat its own purpose if it ghettoised itself, and excluded men. The women argued that the whole point of the "reclaim the night" march was that it was just women. Women are obviously free to walk the streets day and night if they have a male escort. It is when they are alone that they are under threat. Cormac could see that, but the march functioned on a symbolic level rather than a practical one. It wasn't actually going to make the streets any safer for women. It was purely a political gesture, a showing of strength to the public and to the politicians. Jeananne lost her temper with him.

"Yes. The march functions on a symbolic level. And the symbol is of women walking *alone*, laying claim to the night. Now you are just going to have to face this if you want to stay with the group. Certain things are for women only. Right? If you want to be part of our revolution, you've got to give us space."

Cormac went off with a hang-dog look on his face, and arranged to meet them in a pub after the march, this much he presumed he was allowed. The march went from Parnell Square to Kildare Street. A joyous celebratory affair. Candles and music and chanting. Jeananne had the loudspeaker and led most of the chanting. "Whatever we wear, wherever we go, yes means yes and no means NO."

When they arrived at the pub, the general mood was euphoric. Jeananne spotted Cormac sitting in the corner with a puss on him but after some of the women chattered to him for a while he couldn't but get sucked into the mood of the company. Jeananne had a couple of drinks, and this calmed her a little. She managed to avoid Cormac, because she knew that any contact with him would immediately put her in bad humour. She got drunk quite quickly and she started to dance. The pub was mainly full of women from the march. The

52

dance floor was tiny, so her dervish dancing had to be contained.

Unable to relax, Jeananne gathered her things together and left the pub in plenty of time for the last bus. She leant against the bus stop, and felt a sort of general unease. A malcontent was following her around. Happiness never seemed to really happen for her. Cormac arrived at the bus stop, and they nodded at each other. They had never been in this situation before. Alone, and having to ignore each other. It began to rain, yet they didn't comment. Teeming chilly March rain that made other people dash and giggle. They stood there in silence while the rain bucketted down on them in sheets. Great drops were dripping from Cormac's nose. Jeananne could feel a small river forming down the back of her neck.

Cormac turned to her and grabbed her in his arms and kissed her firmly on the mouth. She gasped. He pushed her against the wall and pressed his body against hers, fastening her hips to the wall with his own hips, and grabbing her hair in his fist. Desperately he dug his fingers into her back, and she could feel his hands through her thin jacket. She responded to him. Hungry. Turned on. The rain pelted down and they were both soaked through. He steered her to the road and hailed a taxi. One stopped and they bundled into the back where they devoured each other all the way to Ranelagh. They arrived at his bedsit where, panting loudly and avoiding her eyes, he poured them two glasses of white wine and turned off the light. They sat there, saying nothing, in the darkened room, drinking the wine, both of them breathing loudly. He came over to her and kissed her, passing a mouthful of wine to her which spilled down her cheek onto her neck. Then he bit her neck, hard, and when she cried out, he started to pull off her clothes. They had ravenous, desperate sex. They crucified themselves with desire. As Jeananne drifted off to sleep, she could taste the blood in her mouth where she bit her lip when she came.

Cormac was still wide awake. He could not believe his behaviour at the bus stop. What had he done? Who the hell did he think he was? He hadn't intended to do it, it was completely unpremeditated. God! It was something he'd never done before. If he'd been wrong, he didn't know what she might have done. He'd fancied Jeananne since the first day he met her in tutorial, and he simply couldn't understand her attitude to him. She was much more tolerant of the other guys. He had done a bit of discreet research. Apparently she didn't go out with guys. She appeared to actually dislike men, and was contemptuous of them when the opportunity arose. She was definitely not gay. If she had been, she was the type who would be political about it. Now it seemed that she must have been interested in him all along. Funny way of showing it. As she slept beside him, he thought that she looked as fragile as a small child, just as trusting and just as beautiful.

When she woke up, she was alone in the bed. For a moment her mind was deliciously blank, then she sat up, suddenly shocked. He was seated at his desk, angle-poised lamp turned on and leaning over him like a watchdog. She remembered him saying to someone that he did two hours reading every morning before he went in to college. He claimed to be an insomniac. Jeananne had always reckoned it was a fib, just to make him look glamorous. Insomnia, a real intellectual's disease.

Jeananne got out of bed and pulled on her clothes. He didn't look up from his desk. It was a very long time since Jeananne had been with a man. She lifted up a magazine and slammed it on the ground. He didn't look up. She banged a spoon off an empty cup. He didn't look up. Finally, she thumped a chair off the ground, and he slowly swivelled round in his swivel chair.

"Oh, so you want to talk to me now. You ignore me for six months, but now that I've finally fucked you, you might talk to me."

Jeananne gathered up her things quietly and left the flat. Cormac felt awful. He had opened his mouth and had meant to ask her had she slept all right, but instead all that hostility came out. He didn't exactly know where from.

Jeananne went into college that day, but didn't attend class. Instead she went to the computer lab, and taught herself to type. She got a Wordstar typing tutorial and methodically worked her way through it. This was something she had wanted to do for ages, but hadn't got around to. She concentrated totally on it, sitting at the computer for twelve hours non-stop. By the end of the day she could touch type, albeit slowly. Only when she got home to bed did she think about Cormac and the previous night. And then only for a second. She had difficulty sleeping, so she spent most of the night reading until she finally collapsed into sleep.

The next day she saw Cormac at tutorial. He was nervous and uneasy with her. She was totally calm and controlled. The others in the class noticed that Jeananne was for the first time behaving with civility to Cormac. They were astounded. So was Dr Oestes. Cormac, however, found it unnerving. Everything went smoothly for the first half hour of the class, until a point of dissension arose. Jeananne and Cormac once again laid into each other. The fight was even more vicious now. Jeananne got totally worked up. The rest of the class became very uneasy. It looked like she was going out of control. She wanted to thump him. She walked over to his chair and stood in front of him, her closed fists rigid and shaking. Finally she managed to control herself and sat back down. Dr Oestes asked her to stay back after the class.

"What's the matter, Jeananne?" she asked kindly, knowing that there was something seriously wrong with the young woman. Jeananne smiled and apologised, saying that she just got carried away. That she was beginning to feel a little overwhelmed, and that she thought she needed a good rest. Dr Oestes' kindness almost made her feel upset, but she managed to get out of the room before this happened. She was in a state of total emotional confusion, almost unbearable. Thoughts raced through her brain really fast and seemed to crash into each other and get tangled. Her head felt like it might explode. Outside the door, stood Cormac.

She was going to walk past him, but she didn't. Instead she stood in front of him. He didn't say anything, just put an arm around her and steered her along the corridor, down the stairs and out onto the campus. He took her to the bus stop, where they caught a bus to his place. They still didn't speak. Cormac lit a fire, and sat her into a big old chair, and wrapped a blanket around her. He then made her a cup of hot sweet cocoa. She looked like somebody who wanted to cry, but couldn't. He read her some poetry, and finally she started to relax.

They started to chat. It was the first time they had ever had a conversation. Both were exellent communicators in the formal sense, could get a point across to a large assembly without any bother, but neither could communicate intimately. Cormac started to open up like a flower.

"I came to college in Dublin to escape my family. My father is insane. He doesn't talk. He is cold to his children, and has nothing but contempt for my mother. He talks about her to people like as though she's not there, when she's standing in the room. And she behaves like she's not there. It's as though she's so used to feeling not there that she's become not there. She wanted me to go to college at home in Cork, but I decided to save my own skin and come to Dublin. Sometimes I feel bad about that." There was nothing untrue in this story, but it wasn't telling the truth. He didn't tell her how violent his father was, he didn't tell her how many times he'd been beaten near senseless by him. He didn't tell her that fundamentally he felt sorry for his father, a big distant tragic man who hated himself and all around him because he had been led to believe he was a king and grew up to find he was a hotel manager with a dowdy wife and six kids.

He spoke of his interest in feminism as a way out from the straitjacket of traditional notions of masculinity. Jeananne started to feel for him, to appreciate his stories, and to see where he was coming from. Cormac noticed that it was he who had been doing all the talking, and he asked her to share something of herself with him.

She found it easier to listen than to talk, but she made the effort anyhow. She told him about her interests in women's writing and feminism, about her particular liking for the nineteenth century novel. She spoke elegantly of Simone de Beauvoir. She told him about the time she won a scholarship to go to Stratford on Avon to visit Shakespeare's home town. She didn't tell him about anything really. Cormac knew that she was holding back on him. She told him that she hadn't had a lover for a long time. That she didn't like men. That she enjoyed being independent. That she found relationships disempowering. That night they went to bed and drifted off to sleep in one another's arms, totally peaceful, totally content.

Jeananne and Cormac became a regular couple. Everybody said that they'd seen it coming a mile off. Their sparring matches continued, but they were a lot more good-humoured. Dr Oestes watched the progress of the two with some satisfaction. She had thought they were perfect for each other from the very first day they both walked into her class. They spent a huge amount of time together, and their studies slipped. Jeananne sat a paper for which she was ill-prepared, and only got a third. She was furious with herself, and resolved to concentrate more on her work. A new resentment of Cormac developed.

They had very unusual sex. There was something of an unleashing of furies about it. It was hard to tell exactly when this fury overspilled into violence, and who exactly started it, but both co-operated with it. They never discussed it. It was something that just happened. To begin with it was a simple matter. They played rape games. He was a little reluctant, but Jeananne talked him into it. It gave her a marvellous feeling of power. He would defile himself with his own worst nightmare for her. As he got more used to it, Jeananne could tell that his protests weren't sincere. She knew that he liked it. She hated him for liking it. She didn't exactly like it herself. It was hard to explain. To begin with, the violence was egalitarian, but after a while she became less active, and he became less passive. They both began to hate themselves for doing it, though each managed to put it out of their minds afterwards.

After a period of dormancy, the women's group became quite active again. A campaign was launched to provide better lighting on the lonelier exits from campus. A number of attacks on women had been reported. Jeananne and Cormac were automatically asked to form the backbone of the organising committee. They agreed. A massive drive was launched. This campaign was masterminded by Jeananne, though she kept very much in the background, managing to keep up her studies also. Cormac was to the fore. He was magnificent. His speeches were sharper than ever. There seemed to be an added edge to them. One day she arrived at a meeting with a black eye.

"Shit. What happened to you?" asked one of the other women.

"Oh, Cormac beats me." Jeananne laughed in reply. The whole group laughed with her. Even Cormac laughed. The idea was quite ludicrous. Finally the college authorities upgraded the lighting. Cormac and Jeananne were the toast of the group. Everybody thought they were a great couple. So good together.

Jeananne started to work very hard again. She spent less and less time with Cormac. It seemed no longer necessary to see so much of him now that they'd moved in together. They slept together every night, but otherwise, they only met in class or in the group. Both spent long periods in the library. In the back of Jeananne's brain a discomfort was spreading like cancer. Her conscience was gnawing at her. The dichotomy between her public persona and her private existence was growing unbearable. Cormac seemed to be more and more distant from her. They

hardly ever talked. He rose early to do his two
hours reading in the morning and turned his back
on her. His cold streak resurfaced. He hated her and
he hated himself for what he did to her. They
seemed so civilised during the day, yet at night,
once the lights were turned off, their monsters
emerged under cover of darkness. She loved to
control him. She loved to monitor the amount of
pain. She loved the pain. She found it exciting. It
made her feel more. They never did it with the
lights still on. They needed to hide their shame.
They didn't make love. They made hate. Jeananne
refused to think about it. Everytime the subject came
into her head, she simply thought about something
else. She set herself a rigid study timetable, and
stuck to it meticulously. She also started jogging in
the morning. She worked so hard that she forgot to
eat. Her face grew pinched and dark shadows
appeared under her eyes. Dr Oestes noticed the
change in her, and asked her if she was all right.

"Fine," she said, and she believed it.

The exams were approaching, and they were
working very hard. Both were irritable and uptight.
After a long day in the library, Jeananne came
home to find Cormac sitting alone in the dark. She
switched on the light, and he startled her.

"Turn it off," he barked.

She did so.

"Why do you do it?" he asked. "Jeananne. Why
do you make me do it? Why?"

She stood and stared in the direction of his
voice.

"We could've had a good beautiful relationship. We could have got into the whole cosy thing, sat around drinking cocoa and hugging each other, made each other feel warm and good. Instead, look at what you made me do to you."

"I made you do it? You didn't have to. I didn't hold a gun to your head. You liked it."

"No. I never liked it. I don't know why I do it, but it's certainly not because I like it," and he let out a terrible groan like an animal. "Why do you do it?"

Jeananne knew why she did it. She did it because, in embracing and controlling the monster, she disarmed it. In monitoring it, she conquered it. She liked it because it made her feel. Otherwise she felt nothing.

"I do it because it makes me feel. Otherwise I don't feel anything."

Cormac got up and turned on the light. This was the first time they'd talked about the worm at the heart of them. It was also the first time that they'd produced the worm with the light on. They both blinked at the brightness, and blushed at the sight of each other. They were both naked.

"Jeananne. I think that you should see a psychiatrist. I think you need help. There's something wrong with you, if you like that."

Jeananne got riled.

"Oh mister mentally-healthier-than-thou. And you're the picture of stability. I tell you, I'd rather be the victim in this scenario, than to be so bloody brutalised that I actually enjoyed perpetrating it. Not to mention the sheer hypocrisy of it, you crooning away at our women's group meetings. I don't know how you can live with yourself, never mind with me. You make me sick."

With that she slapped him hard across the face. Cormac didn't react for a second. He just stared at her with his pale grey eyes, unblinking, unflinching. For the first time, Jeananne became actually frightened of him, really frightened of him. He stood there, stiff as a pole and stared at her. Expressionless, he turned and walked to the door. For one terrible moment, Jeananne thought she had failed, that he was walking out. But he stopped at the door, and still speechless, turned out the light.

Once the darkness had re-established itself, Jeananne felt more comfortable. Darkness was where she felt she belonged. She closed her eyes and waited for the blows to fall.

Afterwards, when she embraced him, she felt so powerful. She knew that if the lights were on, that his face would be full of remorse, that he would be crucified with it. She knew that she had reduced him to something lower than he ever thought he could be. She had made him into his own worst nightmare. The ferocious demon that was locked inside him, that shit that he had squeezed into a box, she had managed to liberate. Even now that he had confronted himself over his behaviour, she could still do it. She licked the blood from her split lip, and wondered how she'd cover it up tomorrow. Cormac was shaking now, in her arms, shaking with remorse, and Jeananne was also shaking, shaking with pent-up desire to laugh.

Cormac didn't sleep at all that night. He lay there thinking and thinking. Sometime around dawn, he resolved to leave her. He knew that they would kill each other otherwise. He made the decision and a weight like an anvil lifted off his chest.

When Jeananne woke in the morning, she perceived a change in Cormac. He was no longer ashamed. He wasn't slinking round the flat furtively; instead he was very relaxed, making her a cup of tea. Something was going on. Jeananne watched him for a while, as he pottered around the room.

They both headed off to college. On the way down the road to the bus stop, they passed a man standing on the path with two kids. One child, the little girl who looked about six and wore an oversized red coat, was whinging. It is a noise that would break your heart. The man got tired of her and growled at her to stop blubbering. The tears increased and got louder, and then, out of the blue, the man hit the little girl such a thump, that the child reeled and fell over. The man dragged her to her feet again, and hit her a number of times more, holding her by the shoulder so she wouldn't fall over with the blows. The child's cries increased. The man's voice strained hysterically with a repeated "would you stop that whinging you little bitch". The six-year-old continued to howl. Jeananne and Cormac stood transfixed and watched the scene. A red colour crept up Cormac's neck and spread over his cheeks. Jeananne went over to the man and punched him in the face. This brought the man to his senses somewhat, and Jeananne roared at him.

"How dare you hit a little kid, you big bully. You big shit you. She's so little, you fucker." And Jeananne's voice cracked as she started to cry and belt him again, hysterically screaming at the man, who held up his hands to protect his face from her fury, while the little kid in the big red coat looked up in wonder, momentarily distracted from her own sorrows by the scene before her eyes. Jeananne had gone completely berserk now, she was strong and overpowered the man, and pinned him up against a wall. Cormac came to, and rushed over to restrain Jeananne. The man was as white as a sheet with blood coming from his lip.

"She's mad," he kept muttered to Cormac as Cormac put his arms around Jeananne who started to sob and shake. The kid in the red coat stood on the pavement and, staring at all the adults, rolled up one of her sleeves to fit her little arm. Cormac took Jeananne off to a coffee shop, where she sat in silence for a time and Cormac stroked her hand. Finally she talked.

"Last night I had this dream that I'm always having. I've been having it for years. I'm sitting in Bewley's drinking coffee, and this huge guy comes in and starts to throw shapes around the place, clearly deranged. He has a hunting knife. He picks up this kid, around twelve or thirteen years old and starts to swing her round. The kid screams and screams, and her mother just sits there, with her arms protecting her other three smaller kids shouting 'Somebody do something' or something like that. I sit and watch and I am afraid. The guy then clearly gets sexual with the little girl, and starts to stroke her body in a sexual way, and the girl starts to scream louder and the mother is screaming. Suddenly I stop being frightened, and I go over to him and I say 'Hey, big boy, leave the kid alone.' I am cool as a breeze, totally unruffled. I have a small flirtatious smile on my face. 'Let the kid go back to her ma. She's only a kid,' I say. 'She's no good to you anyway. C'mere, I'll give you a good going over. It'll be the best night that you've ever had. I'm very good at it. Let her go. She'll just be a bother and cry all the time.'

"The madman looks from me to her and back to me again. The kid has stopped crying now. He looks from one of us to the other again, and finally he lets her go, and transfers the knife to my throat and takes me away. As he takes me away, I think how it is that he cannot damage me now, because the damageable bit has been dead a long time. I think of the face of the little kid smiling and playing and maybe someday falling in love and being happy and I think that we can take anything when we are old, because part of us is dead, but we should protect the little children, because it would be too terrible if they grew up like the deserts that we are."

This was more than Jeananne had ever revealed in all the time Cormac had spent with her. It was the most that she had spoken about herself. He held her hands in his and started to cry.

"I know that you're going to leave me," she said. "I could tell by the way that you made the tea this morning. I may be a cold fish, but I'm observant. I don't blame you for leaving me. You're doing the right thing. But remember, I didn't teach you anything that you didn't already know. I just opened the gates. I didn't create the hounds that escaped."

"I know," said Cormac. "I didn't create them either."

Jeananne had calmed now, though the skin on her face felt very tight, stretched from ear to ear over her flesh. Cormac dried his eyes and went up to the counter to order cocoa. He looked down at Jeananne, and was struck by how normal she looked. Just like anybody else, any twenty-year-old student from any university. She looked so normal, you could almost believe she was. At that moment he loved her. Not in the way he had before, tyrannised by desire, but in a new way. In the soft sad way of pity.

They decided to take the day off from college and get the Dart out to Howth. There they would climb the hill and look out over the sea and shout and scream to rival the seagulls in a frenzy of boisterous energy. There they would feel the wind in their hair and against their faces and they would think how small they really were.

Little Mo,
A Phenomenon in Stilettos

Mo looked guilty. She knew exactly what she had done wrong, and that Jenny was furious with her.

"I'm sorry," said Mo. "I know you're cross."

"Please, say nothing," said Jenny, and she went to the drinks cabinet and poured them both a drink. They had shared this flat for two years, and slowly over this time, Jenny had learned that Mo was simply not trustworthy, so why was she surprised about how things had turned out tonight? She should've known better.

Jenny had first met Mo eight years earlier when they were green little freshers studying English in UCD. All the students were shyly finding their feet but there was something in Mo's leather jacket and brazen jaunty walk that attracted Jenny. Mo seemed a person apart. Jenny could remember clearly the first time she was captivated by Mo. It was a dreary drizzly day and Mo came to the tutorial very dressed up, in glitzy clothes and heavy make-up. John Delaney, a very young and very quiet boy in their class, noticed the difference, and complimented her. He said "You look really well in that dress. It's lovely, it suits you," or something like that, the poor innocent. Mo, stared him in the eye and said "Would you ride me?" She said it right there, in front of everyone, including the tutor. People's mouths dropped open. John coughed and spluttered. He blushed crimson, and through the blush Jenny could see that the answer was indeed "Yes, yes I would." From then on, poor John Delaney was at Mo's mercy. Three years later, at a party on graduation day, a more sexually mature Mo seduced John Delaney. When Jenny asked her why, Mo answered, "After three solid years of devotion, he deserved a bit." Mo could be cruel and thoughtless in some ways, but she was the only person Jenny had ever known who would fuck as an act of generosity.

Jenny clued in to Mo's power games, and was fascinated by them. She observed that Mo was a little alienated from herself. It was as though the true Mo inhabited a space two foot over the head of the physical Mo who walked around life performing acts for her amusement, like an obedient slave.

Jenny and Mo were inseparable during their first year at college. They got a flat together and people assumed that they were lovers. At the end of their first year, they each met their first boyfriends. Jenny fell deeply and sincerely in love with a poet two years older than her. She brought him home to meet Mo; shortly after, Mo lost her virginity with one of their lecturers and came home with a hilarious tale about him which had the two girls in kinks for a whole night. It was June the 16th. Bloomsday. He had all this gear in his wardrobe that he liked to dress up in. He took the two costumes out and she made him wear the woman's one. She played Leopold to his Molly. He was nervous to begin with but she slung a few more glasses of wine down his throat and finally got him going. She didn't let him know how inexperienced she was, and he wasn't too keen to find out. Later she amused herself around college by torturing him with vicious and mischievous winks whenever their paths crossed.

From then on, their friendship eased a little. They both needed change. Jenny talked constantly about her lover, Brian, and about his poetry. Mo stayed out a lot. Jenny began to feel left behind. Mo started to feel shut out. As Mo's friends became trendier and more monied, as they assumed a more luxurious air, Jenny began to feel as if she no longer fitted in. It was Jenny who broke away, who decided to leave Dublin and head off to California to do a post-grad. When the two girls parted at Dublin Airport, they were both quite relieved. There was too much undiscussed business between them. Their goodbye hug embarrassed them a little, each conscious of dissembling. As Jenny settled into her window seat high above the Atlantic, Mo dashed from the airport and into her first job interview, which she got. Mo was good with her mouth, expert with her mouth. She was born for public relations.

Three years later, by a complete fluke or some plot of fate, Jenny met Mo on O'Connell Bridge the very day that she returned. The two young women immediately resumed their friendship. Time had changed them both. Jenny had become more confident. She inhabited herself in a much fuller fashion. Aspects of her personality which had been a timid whisper were now a bold statement. Mo too had ripened. She seemed to have over-evolved. She had always had a mischievous playful attitude to her sex life, but now she seemed to treat it like a game. Her lovers were like characters in her personal soap opera. They were just a joke to her. Jenny began to wonder if Mo actually picked men up in order to talk to her friends about them later on in the pub.

Jenny and Mo moved in together for the second time. Neither was quite sure why.

Their new personalities complemented each other. Jenny tended towards introversion and solitude; her frivolous side needed encouragement. Mo kept Jenny entertained. Everything was a huge joke to her. Her penchant for sensory gratification and her desire to fill her life with noise benefited from Jenny's meditative seriousness. Occasionally Jenny would ask Mo "Why?" and Mo would stop in her tracks. Mo wasn't used to asking why. She translated immediate reality into immediate sensation.

The Mick episode was an example of just how emotionally corrupt she had become. Mick started working in Mo's office, and she came home raving about him. Six foot two, dark, perfectly proportioned. She bet Jenny a fiver she'd have him before two weeks were out. Sure enough, she arrived at Marina's dinner party with him on her arm. Sure enough, he was as dropdead gorgeous as Mo had promised. Sure enough, she cornered Jenny in the kitchen while Jenny was helping Marina scoop out the chocolate mousse, looking for her fiver. Mo hung out with Mick for four months. Quite a while by her standards. Whenever they appeared anywhere, people would die laughing. Everybody knew Mo's tastes in men, and Mick was good-looking to the point of ostentation. He was also very quiet and shy, qualities Mo's set mistook for dullness. Mo's trendy friends couldn't understand a person's desire for tranquillity. Jenny was fond of Mick. He was quiet and gentle. Jenny could see a genuine connection between Mo and him. Almost despite Mo, a truly honest affection began to grow between them. But this wasn't what Mo wanted. It wasn't part of Mo's plans. It didn't belong in Mo's vision of the universe.

After the first flush of resuming their friendship had passed, Jenny started to become a little more cautious about Mo. Her friend from college days seemed to have been replaced by a semi-machine. One day, when Jenny came home with a new dress and tried it on for Mo, it suddenly dawned on her that Mo was envious. Mo looked at the dressed-up Jenny with a slightly begrudging smile, begrudging of Jenny's neat and trim figure. There were other occasional little hints. Little things. Mo didn't look delighted when Jenny was offered a highly prestigious job. She playfully resented the time that Jenny spent reading and working in what was ostensibly free time. Jenny stopped trusting her as fully.

Tonight's incident with Damian was an example of the type of thing she might easily do. Jenny very rarely expressed interest in a man, and when she did, it was serious. She couldn't understand how Mo could have flirted so outrageously with Damian when she knew that Jenny was interested in him.

"I'm terribly sorry, Jenny," said Mo.

"What good is 'sorry', when Damian has asked you out?"

"I really didn't mean to do it. I was actually trying to flirt with Peter, but my aim was off."

Jenny couldn't stay angry with Mo for long, a smile broke through. Mo also started to smile. Mo had the most amazing mouth. It was full of teeth. More teeth than anybody else. Her lips were thick and dark. Her mouth was the most expressive part of her face. It was both ugly and beautiful all at once. In a certain light it was almost a deformity. Sometimes her lip would curl up and she looked quite vicious. Other times she smiled and she looked a picture of gentle vampishness.

Mo changed out of her little black dress and into her nightie and wrap. She had begun to put on a bit of weight, but she still looked smashing. She had one of those bodies that seemed to scream SEX. She was only five foot, to Jenny's graceful five foot ten. Whatever she was made of, it seemed to have been compressed and intensified in order to fit into her tiny frame. As the two girls went off to bed Mo gave Jenny's arm a little squeeze. She was genuinely sorry for what she'd done. She honestly didn't think. It didn't occur to her that Jenny would be upset.

The next morning Mo came up with the idea. It was the plan which became known as the great Elephant and Castle date swap. Damian had asked Mo out to dinner, and she suggested the Elephant and Castle. Mo's idea was that Jenny would phone up Peter, Jenny's colleague who was Damian's friend, and ask him to make up a foursome on the same night, and the two women would swap them.

"But what if they don't want to swap?"

"They will. Men never know what they want. You have to show them, honestly."

"I bet you it won't work."

"I bet you a tenner it will."

Jenny agreed to Mo's plan, knowing that it was a little foolish of her. Mo's ways weren't hers, but somehow she often found herself helpless in the face of Mo's persuasive powers.

The Saturday night of the date arrived, and eight o'clock found both girls in a window seat in the Elephant and Castle. Jenny shook like a jelly, Mo was cool as a Caesar salad. Jenny was dressed down, in muted colours, in what she supposed would be suitable to Damian's tastes. Mo was in her high tart, late eighties, neo-nymphette, black and red number. They ordered a bottle of wine and drank a toast.

"To the plan," smiled Mo.

As the glasses clinked, Jenny looked fondly at her friend and suddenly had a sensation that she could see her a little clearer. Mo was laughing and sparkling, like a Christmas tree decoration, but she seemed a little too manic, too desperate, too much. Jenny pitied her.

The two blokes arrived. Jenny could smell brandy from Peter's breath when he kissed her. They had obviously been for a stiffener. Opposite Jenny sat Peter. Peter was a colleague from her office, and she was easy and relaxed with him. Damian was an old friend of his. He was a tall serious-looking man, with a lopsided mouth and a strange grin. He was dressed very formally and, for the first time, Jenny noticed how carefully kept his nails were. Jenny was very attracted to him, in a completely physical way. She feasted her eyes on him. It would be a little difficult to talk to him. She would have to talk across Mo and Peter. This didn't seem to phase Mo though. Flirting diagonally was all in a day's work. Mo moved in for the kill straight away. She bantered skilfully with the very good-looking waiter, a practice she knew would alienate Damian, but tickle Peter pink. Damian, uncomfortable with this, made small talk with Jenny. Jenny discovered that Damian was a keen bridge player; she herself had played bridge since she was a little girl.

The starters arrived, and Damian began to relax, as Mo's mouth, that magnificent mouth, all shiny teeth and glossy lips, tore crabflesh from shell. Jenny watched Mo's outrageous behaviour, amused by the sheer innocence of her expression, as she dug her pearly teeth into the whiter meat. She had both men captivated. Jenny just looked on. She felt helpless and genuine and plain.

The main courses arrived, and Mo played rare steak to Peter's lamb and to Damian and Jenny's vegetarian specials. Jenny swapped some of her artichokes for some of Damian's breaded mushrooms. Jenny could see that the light in his eyes had dimmed a little when he looked at Mo. Extraordinary. She could turn him off as easily as she could turn him on, as if she had found a switch in him. Damian spoke more and more to Jenny. They discovered a cluster of mutual acquaintances, while Peter lost himself in Mo's brown Mediterranean eyes. As they ordered dessert, Peter surrendered his soul to the bundle of appetite sitting opposite him. Over Pecan Icecream, Damian asked Jenny would she like to play bridge with him some time at his club. Jenny delightedly agreed. She couldn't believe it, but the plan was working. Damian saw that Mo had no interest in him, that her one woman show was not being played for his benefit tonight. He couldn't remember what it was that he had liked about her when he first met her last week. She seemed like a different person then, not just mildly different, but radically so.

They finished the meal and walked out into the night. As they made their way through the Saturday night throng towards the taxi-rank, Jenny and Damian fell behind, chattering amiably together. The women took the first taxi and, as it pulled away from the rank, they both erupted into laughter. Uncontrollable peals. As soon as they pulled themselves together, they burst out again. They were practically home before they could talk intelligibly. They fell into their flat, where Mo immediately demanded her tenner wager.

"I did better," laughed Mo. "Peter asked me to go to a concert with him, you only got asked to play bridge."

"Well, I like bridge."

"Do you know what'd be real fun?"

"What?"

"Real, real fun?"

"What?"

"To swap them back!" and Mo collapsed into gales of laughter and tumbled off the sofa and onto the carpet. She rolled over and over, helpless with mirth. She laughed so much she almost choked. For Mo, life was a huge joke, an endless road of laughs. Jenny managed a few chuckles, but she honestly didn't find it quite so funny.

Jenny got up to go to bed, but before she went into her room Mo stopped her. Mo held her wrist and stared her straight in the eyes.

"Jenny, I know I'm bad. I know I'm a dangerous bad person. I've changed a lot since you knew me before. Remember, I used to be so sweet. But I never do it to the weak. I've never done it to someone who couldn't hack it. I know I'm bad. But I am fun. Do you still love me?"

Mo tightened her grip on Jenny's wrist.

"You know I'd be heartbroken if you didn't. I've

always wanted to be like you. Good and measured and well-motivated. But I can't be. Just like you can't be me. Tell me that you still love me."

"Sure I love you, Mo. Who can help loving you?"

The two girls hugged. Then Mo kissed Jenny gently on the mouth. Jenny felt the warm tongue engage hers and it shocked her down to her toes. The soft velvety big lips, and then suddenly the teeth gently nipping her tongue. She stood, transfixed, receiving the kiss, and when Mo eased, Jenny pulled away and went into her bedroom.

As Jenny used her cleanser and toner, she thought about Mo saying that she'd only been asked to play bridge. In all probability that was the extent of it. Damian, frankly, didn't seem that interested. More relieved to have escaped from Mo. Mighty Mo the motormouth. Jenny simply wasn't that good at the game. As sleep came to caress her, she remembered, for no reason, coming home from school as a kid. There was a dark secluded lane she had to pass, and a young boy, thirteenish, her age, came out of the lane looking guilty and furtive, walking fast, carrying about him the mood of someone wishing to escape. After him came a man with a leering grin, who leant against a fence and watched the young boy running away so fast that he stumbled as he looked fearfully over his shoulder. Jenny had never forgotten the smug smile of the man, nor the casual sling of his body as he leaned against the fence. Despite her youth, Jenny understood exactly what was going on. She realised then as now that the world could not be divided into the good and the bad, but rather into the fuckers and the fucked.

As sleep overtook Jenny, Mo's kettle boiled in the kitchen and she made herself a coffee and sat down at the table. Mo stared at her coffee awhile, and then took a sip of its bitterness. If Jenny hadn't been asleep, and had looked on that face, she would have seen no expression at all. Nothing. No clues. Just an empty face. But if Jenny had come in. Mo would probably have grinned and put on the triumphant face of the great Elephant and Castle date swap.

Getting Rid of Him

Getting rid of him was difficult. He kept finishing it. Thirty-two times in eight years he walked out on me or kicked me out of his flat or left me to walk home in the rain. Whichever was appropriate to our particular circumstances at the time. I remember the minutiae of all of them. He used to accuse me of having a tape recorder in my brain reserved for his misdeeds. We'd be having a row and then I'd start reeling off verbatim accounts of his crimes, little details, things he'd said to his mother, things he'd said to a taxi driver one time, but mostly things he'd said to me. Bad things. Things that I didn't mention at the time, but just got stored up in a box in my brain, until the inevitable opening of the box. It was frequently after one of these diatribes that he finished the relationship. But he wasn't serious, neither about the relationship nor about ending it. The first time he finished us, the next day I received a dozen red roses by courier at my home with a little card with two hearts on it saying "fuck you bitch". Are these the actions of a man serious about dumping you? How can you let yourself be dumped by somebody who'd send you a dozen red roses and a card saying fuck you bitch? So this is why I say that getting rid of him was difficult. It wasn't the lack of opportunity, I tell you, I had thirty-two opportunities, it was the lack of a single good one.

He didn't want me, but he didn't not want me. This was the irony of the situation. He didn't know what he wanted, he was the genuine article Irish Male. Didn't know his emotional arse from his psychological elbow. Went to the pub to have a good think about us, after one of my ultimatums, and mercifully the fourth pint clouded his brain sufficiently so he was soon able to think about other more pleasant matters such as Man United and the blonde girl in the other corner of the bar. He didn't know what he wanted, but I did. I wanted to marry him. Not to begin with, but after we were together about three years. I was twenty-three at this stage. When I asked him, he paused, with his pint almost to his lips, and put the pint back on the table. I didn't think that I'd ever before seen anything come between him and his pint. He stared at me in astonishment.

"Why?" he asked.

"I want to have babies," I replied. "Why does anybody want to get married?"

"We're not anybody," he replied.

"It's our nature to breed," I said, "birds do it, dogs do it, it just comes naturally."

"Yes," he replied, "but dogs also shit on the

carpet, besides," he said, "What on earth do you want children for? Where would you put them? On your bookshelves? Who'd mind them when we're in the pub? How could you walk in your high heels if you were pregnant?"

"Chinese women managed to be pregnant with their feet crippled. I'd figure out a way. Anyway, I didn't mean right now, I meant sometime, I'd buy a pair of flat shoes and get into training."

Anyway, we batted on like this for a while, me getting pissed off with him, him applying for Donnelly visas. He moved in with me, but that was inconvenient for him when he wanted to walk out on me, because he had nowhere to go except to his mother's. And that was even more of a difficulty, because at least I wanted to be somebody else's mother, not his. I think he had a problem with mothers, he didn't get on at all with mine, but that might have been because he was a perennial graduate student, doing an obscure PhD in a dusty branch of Philosophy, and my mother suspected that he'd never come to any good. She was right, of course, but I'll never let her know that. My mother could sniff 'em out. She had this way of wrinkling her nostrils whenever me or any of my four sisters brought a fella home. Mrs Bennet wasn't in it. She cried for a week after we'd had a visit from an English boy, son of some millionaires, and the five of us let him escape unsnared.

"Too busy running round Dublin with students and no-hopers," she said.

All my sisters had boyfriends who were the

opposite of my mother's desires. Carol in London's boyfriend was both black and divorced. Sheila's boyfriend was unemployed and divorced. Jane's boyfriend was an anarchist. And my kid sister Kitty was having a relationship with a homosexual. And not just any homosexual, but a homosexual who frequently appeared on national television campaigning for gay rights.

"How can a girl be having a relationship with a homosexual?" my mother asked. "Or is there something I don't know about this homosexual thing?"

Well, Kitty is no ordinary girl. She'd find a way to have an affair with just about anybody.

Back to him. I suppose I'd better tell you his name. His name was and still is Denis Cantwell. "Dinny the divil". We had been together four years, and had split up the preceding Christmas. It was April now. We always split up at Christmas. I was on his list of things to give up for the new year. Booze, fags, Clare. He usually only managed a fortnight with the booze and the fags, but he generally lasted till February 14th with me.

This year was surprisingly long. April. I'd heard he'd left the country. I had started dating another guy, Kieran, or Kevin, I can't remember which, and I'd invited him round to my flat for dinner. We were getting on quite well, if I remember rightly. I thought this guy had definite potential. There we were, just cosy, tucking into our dessert, creme caramel, my flatmate safely packed off to the cinema, when I heard the front door opening. I presumed it was Vanessa back from the cinema, but no, it was Denis, armed with rucksack and a bottle of duty free whiskey. Just back from New York. He walked in my door, at eleven at night. The nerve of him. He did apologise about using the key, but said that he was afraid to wake me up. He begged a floor for a couple of nights, and sat down. What was he doing here when he had a perfectly good mother living nearer to the Airport than I did? He even managed to swindle some creme caramel. I couldn't refuse. There was a huge dish. He and Kieran or Kevin knew each other, they had worked together installing lifts in Germany one summer, and had a great chat. He opened the bottle of whiskey, and the two of them dug into it. I washed up. In retrospect, I wish I'd had the nerve to take Kieran or Kevin off up to bed with me, but I didn't. A first bonk is a delicate negotiation, and I certainly didn't want it witnessed by my last bonk. Then Rebecca came home from the cinema, and Denis was just delighted to see her, and she him. He was always very charming to her. The way to an ex-lover's sofa is through her flatmate.

Needless to say, Kevin or Kieran went off into the night, never to be seen again, and Denis installed himself on the sofa in the front room, and finally graduated up the stairs, slithered his way up to the first floor, and insinuated himself into my bed. He didn't actively solicit entrance to my bed, he gave the impression he was quite happy on the sofa. Even washed up a spectacular amount of times, "not to be in the way". He demonstrated a newfound ability to cook. Flung himself into the kitchen with great zeal. I remember him making the most gorgeous guacamole, having looked up the ingredients in the Chambers Dictionary. He always claimed that the answer to most questions was to be found in the Chambers Dictionary. There was a vacuum in my bed, not to mention in my heart, and how could I resist a man who could find recipes in a dictionary? I grabbed him by the arm one night, and hauled him upstairs. After that, he stopped the spectacular wash-ups and cooking. I suppose he felt he was earning his keep at night. In fairness to him, I will say this. He never promised me anything. I was just a complete eejit. There was no excuse for me. I don't have the dignity of having been deceived. All he ever offered was just the one night. We settled back into our pattern of going out, fighting, and splitting up, and so we entered our fifth year.

I was getting older, though. I was twenty-five at this stage, and not as pliable as I was when I first met him. The frizzy twenty-year-old was being slowly replaced by somebody more serious. The high heels had gone, I had ceased to do cartwheels on the balustrade of O'Connell Bridge for kicks. I had a proper job now. My bounce-back ability wasn't as strong as before, and I started to find the relationship devastating. I know your physical healing ability decreases with age, but emotionally you are supposed to get stronger. This was not the case with me.

In the final three years, the long death rattle of our relationship, he was gone more often than he was there. He'd be gone for months, and suddenly, just when things were happening, he would phone or turn up. I got to thinking that he had an antenna that sensed when I was about to get it together with somebody else. Once, I met somebody very very nice at a party, and the next morning, at nine-thirty, the phone rang. I hadn't heard from him in four months but, before I picked up the receiver, I knew it was him.

And, the strange thing was, I couldn't refuse him. Not that he ever made the first move, but he made the move available to me by being there, and somehow, I always made it. But I no longer fancied him. I was no longer impressed with him. I think it was that I couldn't countenance failure on such a grand scale. Having tried so hard for so long to make it work, I couldn't bear to see it go, though he was no longer the magic boy in the night club, the quick wit in the bar. I no longer squealed with delight in his company. I found him compulsive and boring at the same time. Then, when he was gone again, I would howl. I would howl, sometimes for days, sometimes for weeks. I knew, for self-preservation, I had to get rid of him. But, as I said, getting rid of him wasn't easy.

His last exit from my flat wasn't any different from any of the others. It was the usual. We had a row. I threw my glass of wine in his face, he called me "a mad bitch". The same term of abuse he'd hurled at me in the beginning, eight years

86

previously, and he left me again. I couldn't figure him out. But then, I'm not sure he could figure himself out. Or maybe it was as simple as how he put it: "Life is too short to think about the future". He had a thing about the future. He never bought a ten-journey ticket for the bus into town, because he was never sure he'd be coming back.

He stayed gone a long time. Twelve months. I heard conflicting reports as to his whereabouts. I heard he was in Nicaragua. I heard he was in Scotland. I shrugged, and wished him to be any place but in my brain. I saw a psychiatrist who reckoned I was suffering from low self-esteem. I didn't need a psychiatrist to tell me that.

So you can imagine my surprise when I met him on O'Connell Bridge last week, with a blonde woman who was about seven months pregnant. "This is my wife, Patricia," he said. I could tell by his eyes, darting about shiftily, that he was a little embarrassed. It was like meeting somebody who used to sell the Socialist Worker on the street, and now had a fat cat job with a multinational. He said the words "my wife" almost in a tone of warning, in case I had intentions of jumping on him then and there in the street.

Admittedly I had done that once. It was a couple of years ago and he'd been gone a while. It was midsummer, and I spotted him on Dame Street, obviously working, giving a group of American tourists a guided tour. I had sprung up out of nowhere, and put my arms around him, while he was in mid-flight about Viking Invasions and City Walls. We stood there, kissing and holding one another for an hour. The Americans found it funny to begin with, but eventually got bored looking at us and drifted away. Denis heard later that not one of them looked for their money back or complained about the incident. They obviously considered they got value for money. Denis and I kissing on Dame Street lies in several American holiday snap-shot albums, the only place where our relationship now lives on, incarcerated in a kind of silly legend.

I stared in shock and disbelief at this girl. This usurper. She looked normal, not unlike me in fact, except she was blonde. And she had this happy glowy look, like a sixteen-year-old in the first flush of a first passion. He was holding her hand and she was delighted to meet his Irish friends. She was Scottish. I could tell by the way she talked to me that she knew nothing about me. He was married to somebody who knew nothing about me. They invited me to join them for lunch.

"Clare is one of my oldest friends," he said. "She's been a great support all the years."

The way he was holding her hand, the way he looked at her, I could tell he treated her like Dresden china. He had never, in eight years, held my hand. It wasn't ever a big thing with me, hand holding, but still. My system started to shake, I had never experienced such physical and emotional confusion. I felt something break inside me, something crack, like a whip. I couldn't talk, I just walked away, crossed the bridge, and stopped to lean over the parapet on the other side. I looked down into the fat river.

Slowly the shakes and the confusion wore away. I was terrified at what was to come. I was terrified that I might just fall down there on the spot and disintegrate, melt, cease. I looked around at the people hurrying by. It was rush hour, and people were dashing past to get to their buses and trains. People rushing home to their husbands or wives or lovers. People behaving properly, normally. And I wondered why it is that we all want a mate. What is it about us that makes us want a mate? What was it about all these people rushing, many to unhappy homes, homes they were slaving to support, to relationships they were making work because, having invested so much, to acknowledge failure would be to die? Even Denis, who protested, protested too much. He too wanted it, but not with me. Why did people want to be in twos? What was wrong with threes, or fours? Or marauding gangs? Then I think I started to feel all right again. For the first time in my adult life I thought that I knew something. I picked up my bag and my case and made my way to the bus stop. As I settled myself into the seat on the bus, stupid tears started to flow down my cheeks and I knew that at last I was free.

Audition

Jason politely said goodbye to the receptionist at Digges Lane, a girl he knew from before. He knew he hadn't got the audition.

"Thank you, that was *great*. We'll call you. Bye. *Byee*. Thanks, bye," said the casting director, Marion Clune, with an emphasis on the "great" which had a very particular subtext.

He knew he'd made a hash of the audition. He'd landed short of everything he was trying to do with the piece. He had been trying way too hard, doing far too much acting. The director, a black-clad fat man, who looked like an exotic beetle in his leather jacket, observed him throughout with a hostile stare. He was now going to have to go through a few hours of what he termed "post-audition personality disorder". This disorder consisted of hours of self-doubt and coffee in Bewley's, coupled with the sensation that people were looking at him, then a decision to leave the profession as he got the shakes from the coffee, followed eventually by a decision to go to a bar, just as soon as the hour became reasonably respectable. Reasonably respectable in his book was after three o'clock in the afternoon.

He crossed the river to go to The Flowing Tide. He walked over O'Connell Bridge using the central traffic island. He was afraid that if he walked on the footpath at either side, the river might pull him in. It was a problem he had with rivers. Particularly when they were full and he was empty. The river would be fat today, as it had rained without stop for three days. It was raining now. This was the wettest February he could ever remember. He had a problem with rain and rivers.

It was one of the reasons he didn't like Galway. The river there was fat and rushing. He had to close his eyes to cross the bridges there. The Corrib seemed to be a particularly attractive river to die in. It was rushing and ducking and diving. He knew he was being neurotic, but that didn't make it any easier. He had worked there last summer, in a new play about soccer hooligans written by a little girl from the midlands. No size at all she was. It was amazing, this tiny yoke would come into rehearsal, looking for all the world like somebody's little sister, but when she opened her mouth she commanded complete authority. He liked her. She liked him and wrote him extra lines and a scene. They made an attempt at sex one night, an act of desperation, two lonely souls desperate for something neither was equipped to give. They were awkward with each other afterwards, and Jason had a major bout of finding the river attractive. He had made the mistake of getting digs on the far side of the river from the theatre, so he found it difficult to avoid. One day he crossed the bridge and got stuck halfway, his eye attracted by the incongruity of a school of kayakers, riding the river as though it were an animal they had tamed. The kayakers rushed under the bridge and he was stuck, staring at the empty whirling water. It seemed to be sucking him in, wanting him. He threw it a hostage, a little part of himself, his mother's wedding ring which he wore on his little finger. His mother had bought the ring for herself. She had pretended to be widowed, but really, nobody had married her. She had told him various stories about his paternity, none of which seemed to him to be true. He was glad to be rid of the ring. It was immediately swallowed by the river. He knew that in future he had to be more careful. Frequently he dreamt about Galway, and always in the context of a city bound by a demented river.

Jason sat at the bar in The Flowing Tide and ordered a pint. He took off his wet coat and hung it up. The bar was empty enough, it being the middle of the afternoon. In the corner sat two actors, familiar faces. He had acted with them both at one stage. One, Barry, had no talent, just balls. The other, Simon, had no talent, except the talent to lick arses. They were always together, Barry and Simon, possibly lovers, possibly just so much in love with themselves that it was easy for them to get along. It meant that they could be complete Narcissists without paying the ultimate price of loneliness. He decided not to join them, but to sit at the bar and think.

He was now thirty-three. In the past twelve months he had been busy enough. He had done three stage shows and one smallish part in a big film. This was not a disgrace. It was quite a lot actually. People in the business said to him that he was lucky to be always working. Well, that is, people who did less work than he. The total losers. He was a mid-range loser. A non-winner rather than a total loser. Horror of horrors, an also-ran. For this work in the last twelve months, he had earned less money than he would earn as a starter in the civil service. He was twelve years in the business, and he had to sign on between jobs, couldn't maintain any long-term expenditure like a car, and had absolutely no hope of getting a mortgage. He took a long slug of his pint, and immediately began to feel better. He was not able for auditions. They did him in. They reminded him of the practice of the hiring fair. The fat rich landowners would come to the fair and point their fat rich fingers and say "You, you, you, and you." And the rejected labourers had to go home, a failure to their family or perhaps even worse, to themselves. No amount of justification, no amount of "You were very good, but just not suitable" made it feel better.

His friend, a director called Bob, with whom he discussed the whole business of the cattle market, said that he should go to an audition like a curtain salesman showing off samples, and not take it any more personally than that. How could Bob talk to him about curtain samples, when it was his whole life that he brought to his work? In every gesture was human pain, or human joy, or human something. The reason he went into this profession in the first place was because he didn't want to be a curtain salesman. And there was Bob talking about curtain samples. Jason wanted to hit Bob in the face. It was unjust. Why was it that Bob, who didn't think beyond curtain samples, and directed plays with a leaden, journeyman hand, had the power to hire Jason? Jason had worked with Bob three times, and had observed that Bob was always rescued by his cast. Bob's shows did very well, but only because the actors did all the work. He just roamed into the rehearsal room and picked out colours for the curtains. The fact that Bob often hired Jason was another sign that he was an idiot. And the worst thing was that Jason could not tell Bob what he thought of him. Jason's serf status meant that he had to be nice to Bob. If Bob walked into a bar full of actors, everybody would be nice to him. Jason had nothing but contempt for Bob, but never showed it. Bob on the other hand had an awful lot of time for Jason, both as a friend and as an actor.

Jason took another slug of his pint. He didn't want to get into his Bob groove. His brain had a peculiar habit of slipping into a groove, and obsessing about something for an hour, until he was in a state and upset. He had to actively pull his brain out of certain grooves which were dangerous to be in. The Bob groove was a dangerous one. The river groove was a dangerous one. His mother's death groove was a dangerous one. The sad thing about this brain pattern of his was that it didn't work about positive things. His brain never got into a groove about Spring lambs, or sunrises. The only way this groove business ever got positively channelled was when he was playing a part. He'd get into a character groove. He'd obsess about it, and it made him feel good. He decided he would go and talk to Barry and Simon. Barry and Simon were despicably happy, on their third pint. They were celebrating the fact that they both had got parts in a new film to be shot in Co Wicklow. Jason had also done that audition. He hadn't got the part, obviously, since these two had. He had heard nothing from the film company though. This was another thing. You went and did auditions and nobody phoned you to let you know that you didn't get it. More of the cattle treatment. You'd hear around town who had the part at least a week before somebody from the company let you know that you hadn't. This meant that it wasn't safe to go out. You'd be sitting in the bar, just getting into a good mood on the third pint, when somebody's friend who shared a flat with somebody's girlfriend would tell you that somebody else had got the part. Jason sat with Barry and Simon for a couple of hours. He wasn't really enjoying himself. Barry and Simon were not exactly the brightest bulbs in the bar. They were bimbos.

After four pints, feeling muzzy and unhappy, he

went out into the rain again. Sometimes drink numbed the pain, but sometimes it also numbed the juice. He crossed O'Connell Bridge again, again by the central traffic island. He made his way towards Grafton Street, in search of some sausages. He wanted sausages. He went into Bewley's again, and ordered four sausages with a fried egg on the side to make it look like a fry. He also got a glass of milk. He was sitting there, half way through his sausages, when Bob appeared. Bob was always in good form. He joined Jason with a coffee and doughnut, and then hauled him off to Neary's for a pint.

Jason felt mildly better after the feed.

"I'm thinking of giving up, Bob," he said.

"What?" said Bob. "But you can't. You have loads of talent. You're one of the best actors in town."

"You think that, Bob, but nobody else does. You do use me consistently, and I appreciate that, but nobody else does. And I need more work, my self respect needs more work."

"But you do get a lot of work. You're constantly busy, Jason, by comparison to a lot of people. I've made you two offers that you've had to turn down because of something else."

"They are the only offers in my career I've ever turned down."

"Besides, unemployment is an occupational hazard for an actor. You know Karl Richardson, yeah *the* Karl Richardson. Well I met him two nights ago, and he said that he hadn't worked since last May. And look at him. He's a major name, and he's ten years older than you."

"And that's supposed to cheer me up? I might get to be a failure on a grand scale, rather than the third rate failure that I am now."

"But what would you do, Jason? Acting is your thing. I can't imagine you doing anything else." said Bob, a little wearily. Although he loved the company of actors, he was used to them threatening to leave the profession. When actors got together, one of their favourite topics of conversation was what other career they might be brilliant in.

"I'd make a brilliant barman. Look at your man. I could do that. I played a barman in a show once. Did a week's research in a hotel. I want to be normal. This profession makes me feel like a piece of shit. Promise you won't laugh if I tell you the next thing?"

"I promise," said Bob.

"I'm afraid of women. I go to bed with a girl, and I find I just can't get it together because I'm afraid I'll get her knocked up. And if I did get her knocked up, I wouldn't be able to look after her because I'm a bum of an actor who earns less money than a part-time messenger boy."

"You're drunk."

"Yes, but that doesn't mean I'm talking shite. I want to be normal. I want to get married, I want to have a house, and kids. I want to feel like I'm in the world, not outside it. What woman would have me, if I can't look after her?"

97

"Jason, this is really old-fashioned. Women these days don't expect to be looked after. The mots these days would sneer at you if you wanted to look after them. Jason, you're off your head. What century have you beamed yourself in from? There's all sorts of women's lib rights, maternity leave and everything these days. Nowadays they want you to be able to make a damn good chicken curry and appear eager to perform cunnilingus."

Jason should have known that Bob wouldn't understand. Bob never understood anything. He had no sensitivity.

"But what if you disable the woman, by getting her knocked up? Some fucker did that to my mother. Got her knocked up and didn't look after her, the bastard."

"Who the hell did that to your mother?"

"My father, obviously."

"Who's your father?"

"I don't fucking know. I told you. He didn't look after her. I have my suspicions that he was an actor."

"Why?"

"Because it seems like a particularly actory type of thing to do. I also think that I am an actor because of a dodgy gene, and I saw no evidence of it in my mother, so it must have come from my father."

"Jason, you are very pissed now."

"Promise you won't tell anyone."

"I promise. Now I think you should go home and get some sleep."

Bob walked Jason home. They crossed the canal at Ranelagh Bridge, and Jason was so preoccupied he had none of his usual desire to throw himself in. The canal didn't have quite as hypnotic an effect as the rivers had. But it had its own quiet attractions. So calm and tranquil. You would rest in peace there. Bob and he parted on the corner. They lived relatively near each other. Jason went in the door to his flat, and was hit with a blast of cold air from within. His flat was colder inside than outside. He felt the most awful February chill.

The post had come while he was out. The post in his area was erratic. Sometimes it came at eight in the morning, sometimes it came at three in the afternoon, and sometimes it never came at all. There were four letters. The first was from the film people who had hired Barry and Simon, telling him he hadn't got the part. The second was from his agent, telling him that she was thinning her books, and he was "unfortunately" for the chop. The letter was obviously a form letter that she had sent out to all the no-hopers on her list, but she had hand scrawled "It breaks my heart, Jason. Love always and forever. Sharon P." at the bottom of the page. At first he was touched by this, then irritated. The third was a fuck-off letter for an audition he'd done months ago. It had been sent to his previous address, and had obviously sat there for several months before some genius decided to forward it. A fair crop of fuck off's. In what other profession would you invite abuse through your letterbox?

Would abuse follow you from your previous address into your new flat? The fourth letter was from the local library threatening to repossess his overdue copy of *Desperadoes* by Joe O'Connor. He put all the letters in the fireplace and burned them. They didn't give off much heat, just a brief bright flame. An ephemeral blast, then ashes. He went into the bathroom for a piss.

After he pissed, he went to the bathroom cupboard. He kept several packets of paracetamol there. He didn't like to ever feel that he was trapped in life, liked to be positioned near the exit. He was the same in cinemas and theatres. Always chose a seat which was near a fire exit, just in case there was a fire or the show was terrible or he wanted to get home to his paracetamol. He poured himself a glass of water and sat down at the kitchen table. One by one he took them, eighteen in all. Down the red lane they went. He wondered how long it would be. He decided to put on the kettle and wandered around the room.

His attention was caught by the blinking light on the answering machine. It blinked twice, which meant that there were two messages on it. He pressed play. "Hi! This is a message for Jason Duff from Marion Clune. Thanks a million for auditioning this morning. You were fab, David loved you, and the part's yours. Get back to me asap so we can firm up details. Or should I call your agent? Look forward to working with you. Bye bye. *Byeee.* Bye."

And then there was a loud Beep! and the

second message. "Hi Jason. This is Sharon Purcell. Eh, I've just had a call from Marion Clune to say you've got the part. David loved you. So, I've started negotiations. If by chance you got a letter from me about eh, well, eh, just disregard it. Love you. Ciao!"

Jason giggled. David loved him. David the overgrown beetle who sat through the audition with a sour puss on him that'd turn cream. What the hell was he to do now? The part was very attractive. A major break. Why had he been out on the beer all afternoon, instead of sitting at home waiting for the phone to ring? He had sat at home waiting for the phone to ring so many times, except this time. This one right time. He had got ideas above his station. He had forgotten that it was an actor's lot to sit by the phone. It was part of the masochism of the craft. Now what was he going to do about all those paracetamol? He knew he had to act fast. He wanted to play that part. He'd kill himself afterwards.

He decided to phone Bob, who only lived five minutes away, and ask him to come round and sort everything out, get him pumped or something, and accept the part, say he'd be in on Monday, and that he had to attend to a family illness in the meantime. Bob wasn't there, just his machine, with the silly jingles. Fuck. Bob wasn't home yet. He left a message on the machine anyway, asking him to come over, and saying that it was an emergency involving paracetamol. He thought then that he'd better dial 999, or else the Samaritans. He decided in favour of the Samaritans. They'd be more sympathetic to his plight, and he really wasn't in the form for anybody giving him grief, so he started to look them up in the book. The doorbell went. Shit. This was really putting him off his stride, but he decided he'd better open it. He had no idea how long before the paracetamol took effect, but he had a hunch that it would be any minute now.

He opened the door, and there stood Bob.

"Hi Jason. I decided you were too miserable to be left alone, so I went to the off-licence and got us some cans of beer."

"You didn't get my message?"

"What message?"

"I'm fucked. I've got the part in the David Cunningham film. But I've taken an overdose of paracetamol."

"You've what? You've taken an overdose because you've got a part?"

"No, I took the overdose before I played the answering machine, so I didn't realise I'd got the part until after."

"Shit. You should always listen to your answering machine immediately you come in the door, Jason!"

"Sort everything out, Bob, please."

"Jesus. You spend the afternoon with me, and then you go home and try to top yourself. How do you think I feel? And shit, Jason, what are you trying to do? Who would I talk to if you snuffed it?"

"Just sort me out, Bob. Please. You're a pal. Get me pumped and get me the part."

Bob went over to the phone and phoned the emergency services. They said they'd despatch an ambulance straight away.

"And Bob. The details of the film are in my diary, and the message is still on the machine. You're to secure me that part. I don't want to wake up pumped with no part."

"Would you shut up about parts? We're talking about your miserable stinking life here. Don't talk to me about parts."

"And Bob. It's not like showing curtain samples. An audition cannot be like showing curtain samples. It's your whole self you put into it," mumbled Jason, weaker now.

"I never said it was like curtain samples. It was carpet samples. Carpet, not curtain. Now how many carpet salesmen are killing themselves because their rugs get rejected? None. You've got to get a bit more laid back about this carry on because otherwise . . ."

And Bob's voice was drowned by an ambulance noise and a thick black fog.

Dead Wood

I remember the first time I laid eyes on you. I noticed immediately how attractive you were, despite the dowdy costume, and muted persona you had on. You were desperately sexy, almost despite yourself. You didn't quite engage my heart that time, you did interest me though. I told my then boyfriend Thomas that I had seen you, and he teased me about you for a while. That was in 1983. Thomas has since become a fully fledged accountant, and lives in London, in Wembley. He married a girl called Susie, though he still sends me Christmas cards.

The next time I saw you was in Paris in 1985. It was quite by accident. I hadn't realised you were in the film, which I went to, knowing nothing about it, merely dashing into the shady warmth of an afternoon showing on a rainy day. Shortly after the credit sequence, you emerged on the screen. It was funny. It was like looking at an old friend. I smiled to see you, and you smiled back at me in a close-up shot. You smiled back at me. People would probably say that I was being fanciful, that it was just coincidence, but they are wrong. I believe that shot was taken, albeit six months previously, purely for the purpose of my witnessing it on a rainy Wednesday during a brief Parisian holiday. Destiny. You either believe in it or you don't.

I sort of forgot about you then for a while. I returned to Dublin, went back to my usual pattern of trying jobs, and only lasting in them for a maximum of six months, all the time trying to write. I wrote a novel, and sent it to Mills and Boon. They liked it, thought it was really very good indeed, sent it back to me. They wanted a bit more raunch in it. I always meant to get around to injecting the raunch, but never did. I wouldn't admit it at the time, but I think I never finished it because I got involved with Richard, and that became my whole life for a while. I forgot about you. Richard was a handful. My relationship with him was an attempt to alleviate my misery, rather than a positive step in the pursuit of joy. He was separated. His wife had run off with a Mediterranean Eurocrat. He was hopelessly trying to cope with fathering five children, as well as holding down a pressurised job. I stepped into his life like a fairy godmother, and organised him and his kids into a ship-shape efficient home. Those kids were smashing. Things went along fine until I realised that Richard was having affairs behind my back. I never could figure out who he thought he was. While I was minding *his* children, he was off gallivanting with floosies. People can be very ungrateful. I was sorrier leaving the kids than I was leaving him. I still send them Christmas cards.

It was shortly after that, I remember being in the middle of a chocolate binge to cheer myself up, when I next went to the cinema to see you. I was on a date with a nice boy I had met on the 46A. He had boarded the bus at Stillorgan, and sat beside me, squashing the flowers which I was bringing to my mother. He insisted on replacing them when we got to the terminus at Dun Laoghaire, and then he asked me out. It was his suggestion to go to your film. This time you erupted onto the screen in an orgy of you-ness. You had put on some weight, all in muscle. Your body was a thing of immense beauty. I experienced a sensation of lust so pure that it was quite spiritual. I looked at you as you spread yourself across the wide screen, and I decided that not only did I want you, but I would also have you. I looked from you to the 46A boy and back to you again. He didn't compare. I had thought he was cute, but then, everybody is cute if you are desperate enough. When you kissed that other woman in the film, I experienced a pang of jealousy so acute, that I could hardly breathe. I cannot remember what the film was about at all. Neither the storyline nor the other performers impressed themselves on my brain. I lived only in your presence, only when you emerged and flickered across the screen. The next day, I went again and sat through three showings. When I finally came out into the rainy night, and caught my bus home, my life seemed to have assumed an even more profound emptiness, because it did not contain you.

I didn't sleep for three days. I was between jobs at the time, and I sat around in my housecoat thinking of you. I imagined everything about you, what you would be like to talk to, the feeling of the skin on your hand against the skin on mine as we would walk along Dun Laoghaire pier. I never imagined what you would be like in bed. It seemed a bit sacrilegious. My friends all began to get a bit anxious about me, about my apparent lethargy, and my refusal to go out anywhere. They feared me depressed again. They were all wrong of course. I wasn't in the slightest bit depressed. On the contrary, I had never been happier in my life.

I bought all the movie magazines and filled myself in on all the details of your life that were available to the general public. I read of the women stars that your name had been linked with, trying to find a pattern in your tastes. There seemed to be one link, all the women were strong-minded individualists, their careers noted for quality and judgement, rather than quantity. I would have to work on that. I am simply not a careerist, by any stretch of the definition. I have a career in catering. Not only professionally, but ordinary everyday catering to other people. My boyfriends, my sick mother, the elderly lecherous gentleman in the flat downstairs. My personality was never any great shakes. I was never particularly impressed by it, nor was I attached to it. It would be no trouble for me to throw it over in favour of a more adamant nature. I bought a book about assertiveness, and got a hairstyle to match. An assertive hairstyle. A FUCK OFF AND MIND YOUR OWN BUSINESS hairstyle. One with dangerous angles and corners in it. A far cry from the limpy lanky perms I had favoured in the past. There was no messing with this hairstyle. This hairstyle meant business, and so did I.

One day I spent an hour looking at myself in the mirror with no clothes on. It was a sorry sight. My thirty-two-year old body had really been let go to ruin. There were bulges here, lumps there, unnecessary tyres here and there. I enrolled in a gym. I gave up cream cakes and fried eggs and got seriously into trimming the bod. I threw out my drafts of romance novels, and wrote screenplays instead. I worked obsessively. All day and all night for a week at a stretch, a rest for a while, then I'd start up again. I sent them off to various companies both here and in the UK. I think it was the ninth screenplay that got accepted. The BBC editor to whom I sent it entered it for a competition for debut writers. I won. I was flown over for meetings with the director and the producers. Newspapers did profiles and articles about me. The BBC commissioned another full-length drama from me, which I completed in four days, but sat on for a fortnight, afraid to seem too hasty. When I wasn't writing, I was in the gym. Losing weight is a difficult process for me, but I came down from my mountainous size 14 and headed confidently for a 12.

With my first cheque from the Beeb, I went into Brown Thomas and bought a little black dress in a size 8. I told the assistant it was for my sister, who was my height, but much slimmer. It was a beautiful dress, covered in hand-sewn glittering beads. I bought a pair of black stilettos also. These garments I packed in a box with pink tissue paper and put on the top of my wardrobe. Finding earrings to match my fuck off-haircut was difficult. My normal gypsy dangling affairs looked hopeless. Eventually I spied a pair of crescent-shaped ruby clusters which were perfect. I packed these away too.

My second television play, *Seduced,* was a major hit. It was based on an incident that happened to my friend's boyfriend when he was young. It was a great story. Just the right amount of pathos, right amount of violence, right amount of sex. Those that know marked me as *the* emerging pen to be watched. I spent more time in London. Photos of me appeared in the gossip pages. Once there was a photo of you just above the photo of me. You looked divine. I looked well also. It was a good shot of me. You were with a woman, a singer I'd never heard of. I wondered, if you saw the magazine, would you notice me? You probably didn't dirty your magnificent hands with anything as tarty as gossip pages.

I ate nothing but an apple a day for two weeks, and that did it. I got down to ten stone! My old friends in Dublin couldn't get over the change in me, in my appearance and in my career. Airhead

Cora had made it. Who would have thought? Without you, it all meant so little to me.

Shortly after I broke the ten stone mark, I met Robin. It was on the British Midlands 9.30 flight from Dublin to Heathrow. He had the misfortune to be seated next to me when I had one of my frequent mid-flight panic attacks. I grabbed the wrist next to me when the shakes came on and I explained breathlessly what was the matter. He talked gently to me all the way over, and didn't stop soothing until we were safely on earth once again. He was a tall and gentle man. Full of kindness. Worked as a doctor in a large hospital. As I allowed myself to be coaxed into his Battersea bed three weeks later, I forgot about you and felt the warmth of his body. I slept soundly and peacefully in his arms. In the morning when I awoke I looked at him asleep beside me and tried to feel, but you came rushing back to me in all your glory. As we coupled I closed my eyes and imagined you and it almost worked. From then on I stayed with Robin on my trips to London. We achieved a sort of cosiness which was rewarding to us both.

Since I had lost all the weight, my breasts began to sag. I decided to get them seen to. Robin was appalled. He felt cosmetic surgery was a sin against medicine. But I wasn't going to let saggy boobs stop me. If it doesn't work for you, cut it away. Dead wood. I wore a big baggy jumper when I first saw Robin after the surgery, so he wouldn't immediately notice. My new breasts were magnificent, or would be when the bruising healed. They were gorgeous cheeky gently rounded breasts. I had lost all sensation in the nipple. I slept with my back to Robin that night, successfully avoiding his detection of my new breasts. A few days later he discovered them. I was in the bathroom, trying on the black dress and stilettoes and earrings, as I felt the time was drawing near. It was a dress that revealed the shape of the breasts beautifully, though it was still a little too tight for me. Robin came home unexpectedly from work, and caught me. He had never seen the dress before. At first he smiled and I could tell that he thought I looked well. Then his expression changed when his eyes fell on my radically altered breasts. He put his arms around me and he wept. His weeping touched me, kind of.

Finally Robin forgave me for my act of "vandalism" because he had no choice. He had to forgive me because otherwise he would have to walk away from me, and he didn't possess the courage to do that. Meanwhile you were filming in New York, and then you took time off to rest. I read in the papers that you were exhausted. That the last gig had been a tremendous strain on your already exhausted nervous system. You had been working too long and too hard. I feared for your health and felt really strongly that you needed me. Robin was beginning to get difficult. He said that I was cold to him, that I seemed to shut him out. One time Robin was making dinner for us and he was particularly agitated. As he tossed the salad he asked me to make a commitment to him. I nearly told him about you, just to explain myself, but I changed my mind. I told him I couldn't give him a commitment. He said he couldn't go on. Poor Robin. Poor gentle good Robin. Where were all the Robins when I was floundering about in my early twenties? Where was he when I would have had him? But he wouldn't have looked at me then, drippy dangling creature that I was. He loved me now, this creation produced for you. Poor Robin. He thought me cold. I was never cold to him. All I needed to do was close my eyes and think of you and suddenly I was hot as hell. Robin demanded either an agreement from me to marry him, or else that we would split up. He said he couldn't take it anymore. When he finished tossing the salad, he pulled a chair over to me, took my hand in his and rubbed my fingers. I looked at him and felt such an amount of pity. There would always be people like Robin. Willingly playing the slave to the Ice Queen. He walked into it. I didn't enslave him, he enslaved himself.

Finally I decided to tell Robin about you, and that I was going to get you just as soon as I was ready. By the expression on his face I could see everything falling into place. I could see him suddenly understand the boob job. He went mad. He broke things, and slammed out the door into the rainy night. It was the first time I had ever seen Robin out of control. I took out the copy of Sky Magazine containing the article about you. I read it over and over. I looked at the photographs of you from all angles, and kissed the large one before I went to sleep.

Robin came in drunk at about three in the morning. He told me he'd been over with Louise, his ex-girlfriend. I knew the poor sod was just trying to make me jealous. I secretly wished he had a good time with her, but I knew he wouldn't. Robin sleeping with Louise was more a punishment for him than for me. He took sex very seriously, and deceiving somebody in bed would be very hard on him. Tomorrow he would hate himself, as well as hating me.

The next morning I weighed myself and I was nine stone. I tried on the black outfit again, and it was very nearly perfect. I phoned Sonja, my agent, and told her that I wanted an invite to the premiere of your film. It was in two weeks' time. She said she'd get it organised. As the two weeks passed, I stepped up the intensity of my training. I was in the gym every morning instead of every second one.

I spent four hours getting ready. I had bought a beautiful silk underwear set. I shaved under my arms. I applied wax to my legs to remove the hair. It was a painful process, I had never tried it before. It was worth it when it was finished. Physical pain doesn't live long in the memory, it fades away fast. I plucked my eyebrows and I applied make-up to my face. Once I put on the dress, I had to agree with myself that I looked stunning. I looked exactly as I wanted to look.

Sonja called by with a half an hour to spare so

we sat and had a glass of wine. I suddenly began to get nervous, and I told Sonja about you. Sonja laughed and said she was terribly surprised. She had always thought I was too hard-nosed to harbour such romantic notions. She said she'd get me an introduction to you. She knew your agent really well. We arrived early for the screening, and once more I experienced ecstasy as I watched you move across the screen. How could it be that you were so beautiful? You were outrageously beautiful. Like nothing on earth. Like something from heaven. Your body; the way you moved your body was like the movement of a deer in the forest.

You were standing beside a rubber plant when Sonja introduced me to you. We shook hands, your clasp gentle but firm, mine slightly firmer. I knew that these five minutes were the ones that would count. I thought I was making a good impression, but it was hard to be sure. We chatted lightly about a few ordinary things, until you were whisked away by somebody else. I wanted to do something extraordinary, to make sure you would remember me, but I couldn't think of anything appropriate. Instead, I just nodded goodbye, as my whole life went to talk to someone else. You looked over your shoulder at me after you'd left, and it was that look in your eye that made me sure I had you. I recognised it from the screen.

I decided that was enough for tonight, and I would leave you in peace, but start bumping into you by accident in your usual haunts in Soho. It was not a great beginning, but it was a good beginning. I was only half surprised when I answered the phone to you two days later, and when you asked me to meet you for a drink, it seemed like the most normal thing in the world. When we first kissed, I swear my dead breasts felt something, felt something stir.

I am Yoko Ono

The first time Bernard saw the Lizzards, he thought them spellbinding. A group of beautiful women, with a startling chemistry. He sat among the crowd, who nodded and swayed to the music with obvious familiarity. He had just moved into the area, just bought a house there, and Maguires was his new local pub. He was amazed to find that an unheard of band called by such a silly name was so good.

The Lizzards were a hot all-female band. Lela, Mop, Mary and Sharkey. Lela was the singer/ songwriter. Mop the lead guitarist/songwriter. Mary the drummer and main mover behind the scenes. And Sharkey the fiddle player and total flakehead. They had started three years before, doing numbers in the Coral Bar, a small pub round the corner from Maguires. It was Mary who rounded them all up, got them together, dusted them down, made them practice, slept with the owner of the bar so they could do the gigs. She had hauled Sharkey out of a mental hospital; lured Lela away from a marriage to an eco-freak who wanted to live with Lela and a goat in County Clare; coaxed Mop out of her father's shop and into the band. Mary was practical, like her name. She managed the few bob they made at the door, covered the costs, paid the exorbitant rates of the sound man, and doled the girls out pennies for pints. As time passed, they built up quite a following. Soon the Coral Bar wasn't big enough for them anymore. They moved to Maguires, and started to display colour posters. They had a bank account. After the gigs, they sat around in the bar and dreamed of the big time. Talked about tours, about television, about record deals. Mary fuelled them all with her big talk.

Mary shared a flat with Mop. They went round all the time together, partnered each other on social occasions, jointly prepared dinner for guests. Something Mary couldn't share with Mop was the songwriting. Mary simply couldn't write anything, so she stayed downstairs making plans, while Mop and Lela worked on the songs upstairs in Mop's bedroom. She was occasionally a little bit jealous, especially when Mop and Lela would come out of the bedroom, transported with delight by something they'd written, looking for all the world like post-coital lovers. Sometimes Mary would get a piece of paper and try to write a song, but nothing would come out. Just lists, lists of towns and venues and hire companies. Instead, Mary spent time cheering Sharkey up and frightening away Sharkey's demons. Sharkey was like a big kid. She had few of the inhibitions of an adult. She said this was because she was mad, and didn't have to pretend to conform, like everybody else. She could get away with being herself. For a mad person, Sharkey talked a lot of sense. Frequently Lela and Sharkey would crash out for the night in Mary and Mop's house, after the four of them had sat in front of the video machine, watching movies and drinking beer.

They were an odd bunch when it came to romance. Sharkey was very attractive in a waif-like way, but she outweirded anybody who was interested in her. Some unfortunate bloke would fall in love with her delicate fingers and her little body which swayed to her own beautiful music, and think that she was a fragile bud that needed protecting. What a land they got. Once she asked a brand new lover could she watch him make love to somebody else because she wanted to feel the pain, and the poor boy just stared at her. Mary gave out to her for such things. But Sharkey had a kind of a logic which outfoxed Mary. She insisted that "there is nothing weird about wanting to feel pain. I have a lot of pleasure in my life, the music and so on, so I need to feel some pain occasionally in order to remind myself that I am alive." Sharkey was a little black cloud going round the place, looking for somewhere to rain.

Lela had almost married David, the eco-freak. She claimed afterwards that he had put a spell on her, some essential oil stuff he used to put in her bath, and she couldn't think straight. She cited her packing her stilettoes to go and live on a goat farm as evidence that she had been stark raving mad at the time. In fairness, she was somebody who went a bit bonkers when her hormones were up. She fell in love a lot, at least four times a year, and made loud commitment noises shortly after she knew a bloke's name. She'd go round the place imagining what their kids would look like after knowing somebody a fortnight. One of her favourite hobbies was doodling wedding dresses. She doodled millions of them, and compared them to one another. And she wasn't a bit embarrassed about it. Happily showed them to everyone. Her drawing style was good, as she had studied fashion design for a couple of years. After each of her relationships broke up, she would come round to Mary and Mop's house and weep for two hours. After that she would be grand, and want to go out on the tear again. By evening she'd be in love with somebody else. It was all go with Lela. These love affairs were a bit silly in themselves, but they actually contributed a lot to Lela's songwriting abilities. Lela, who sounded like a complete eejit when she whinged in Mary's front room, would break your heart when she sang those sad love songs on the stage, her big grey eyes staring out from under her black fringe.

Mop had had a couple of serious relationships in the past, all of which had worked out badly. One lover had run off with her best friend, another had committed suicide. She was quite happy without anyone, didn't feel she needed more than the companionship of Mary and the gang. She had never particularly liked sex, not for any real reason, but just that she wasn't pushed.

Mary was offhand with men. She was at her happiest down in the pub with the girls, but she liked to have a man stashed away somewhere so she could call on him whenever she felt like a bit. Men weren't very important to her. The real action was with the girls and the band. She was attractive in a very classical way, tall, statuesque, strong-featured. Whenever she was doing a line with anybody, she liked to keep him very separate from the girls. Wouldn't let him come to gigs, never brought him back to her and Mop's flat, but always stayed over with him in his place.

Bernard went home after seeing the Lizzards, and wondered why he had never heard of them before. They were quite startling. He was a journalist, worked on the news desk of *The Irish Times*. The next day at work he couldn't get them out of his mind, so he sought out Larry Marsh, the rock correspondent.

"Yeah, yeah, I've seen them. They're very hot. If you read my part of the paper, you'd have heard of them. I tipped them last year as the hottest newcomers." And Larry mooched off down the corridor. Larry looked like a rock correspondent. Groovy, grungey clothes. By comparison, Bernard looked like an accountant. Well-dressed, well-groomed. Always wore a shirt and tie. There was something anachronistic about his appearance.

Shortly afterwards he realised that two of the group, Mary and Mop, lived at the bottom of his road. He started to see them around everywhere, in the off licence staggering under the weight of a crate of beer. In the Spar shop, buying spaghetti and Ragu sauce. In the cafe, eating buns. He once spotted Mary shoplifting. He became a regular at their Friday night gigs, felt himself drawn there. He didn't intend to be a regular, but it happened despite himself. He would set off to go into town to the cinema, but change his mind and sidle into Maguires. The band got to know him by sight. He looked a little out of place in their crowd, who were mainly younger than him, a lot less well dressed, and generally came in groups. He was always alone. They referred to him as Mr Bailey's Irish Cream, because that was what he drank.

He had been going to see them for several months when one evening, Larry Marsh came in and joined him. "Out scouting," Larry said and the two men settled to enjoy the gig. At the end, Mary came over to them. She was nice enough to Bernard, but chatted up Larry with the finesse of a real pro. Bernard could see what was going on, and was quite impressed. Larry, a victim of his own self-importance, didn't quite appreciate the subtleties of Mary's charm.

"Where did you get the name? The Lizzards, it's kind of odd," asked Bernard.

"I'm sure people thought The Beatles was an odd name," Mary gave Bernard a bored look. He was neither useful nor flashy, so she really saw no point in him. Mary was used to making snap decisions, and once she had decided this about

Bernard, she saw no need to give the matter much more thought. However, when Mary invited Larry back to her flat for a drink after the gig, she did include Bernard in the invitation.

Mop took a fancy to Mr Bailey's Irish Cream immediately. They chatted together for most of the night. A week later, they met by accident in the launderette. A month later they ended up in bed. Though Bernard's house was much more glamorous, Mop insisted that he stay over with her as often as she stayed with him. Bernard complied, but he told her that it didn't take a genius to figure out that Mary didn't like this arrangement.

"Well, that's just tough on her. I do pay half the rent, and I know that Mary organises the band but she can be a bit of a bully, it's not good for her to have everything her own way."

"Suit yourself," said Bernard. But Mop didn't have to endure Mary's doleful eyes. Mary was openly rude to him, and he hated going there, but he did it to keep Mop happy. He would do anything to keep Mop happy, and he was aware that he was being quite successful at keeping her happy. Her wet shining eyes peeping out from under her mop of hair told him that. Mop developed an appetite for sex which surprised her. She couldn't get enough of it. She enjoyed herself with Bernard much more than she'd ever enjoyed herself with anyone before. It might have had something to do with the trouble he took. He spent several hours obsessively pleasuring every little bit of her. He went to endless lengths to spoil her body, and she responded, she very much responded.

One night, Bernard was staying in her flat, and Mop went down to get herself a glass of water after her fifth orgasm. Thirsty work, orgasms. Downstairs, she found Mary, with cotton wool in her ears, slugging from a whiskey bottle. Mary started when Mop entered the room.

"What are you doing up at this hour?" asked Mop, purring from every pore. Mary stared coldly at her for a moment.

"How do you think I could possibly get a wink of sleep, with you screeching like a cat up there?"

Mop thought she was joking, and rubbed her eyes and laughed. She slowly began to realise that Mary was livid. Mary's face was white, and her hands were shaking.

"Shit, Mary, I'm sorry, I'd no idea you could hear us. My God, this is terrible. Do you drink whiskey every night Bernard stays?"

"No. Sometimes I go for a walk, sometimes I put on my walkman and turn the volume up full, and sometimes, yes, I sit down here with earplugs and drink whiskey."

"But why didn't you tell us, we would have stopped."

"I don't like to be a party pooper. Besides, I thought it was really up to you to ask me if I minded you bringing Mr Armani Jackets home every other night. I do live here, and it does affect my environment."

"I didn't think it was beyond the bounds to bring a man home at night. It was something that my mother used to prevent me from doing, but I'm damned if I'm going to let you stop me. I'm sorry about the noise though, I didn't realise it carried. I'll quieten it in future."

Mary smiled sweetly. All the rancour was hidden. "It's all right, duckie, I'm sorry to make such a fuss. It's just the lack of sleep that's getting to me, and it would be a shame to quieten that lovely noise."

Mop returned to her bedroom with her glass of water to find that Bernard had heard every word of the conversation, and was threatening to return to his own apartment that very minute.

"She's a bad lot, Mop. She simply can't stand the sight of me. There's no point in dragging me back here for the night when it obviously pisses her off. It pisses me off too, and I've a perfectly good empty flat less than two minutes up the road, where we'd piss nobody off."

"We'll probably stay there in future."

"I am Yoko Ono," said Bernard.

"What do you mean?"

"I mean that when John Lennon started going out with Yoko Ono it basically broke up the Beatles. Yoko Ono's arrival split up the love affair between John Lennon and Paul McCartney."

"What are you talking about? Myself and Mary aren't in love. We flirt with each other on stage, it's all part of the act. She has lovers all the time."

"Aha! Absolute proof. She has lots of lovers, but

you're the important one. You can tell by the way that she looks at you that she's in love with you."

"Bernard, don't be daft. We're rock musicians, and we're into everything. If Mary and I wanted to shag, we'd've shagged long ago. The fact that we're the same gender wouldn't stop us, it would only encourage us, make us feel kinkier."

"You talk about love as if it were a simple matter," said Bernard.

From then on, Mop stayed over with Bernard almost all the time. She didn't move her stuff out of Mary's though, and kept up her share of the rent. She didn't fancy actually moving in with Bernard. It would have been a bit serious. Mary found herself a new boyfriend, Brian. The Brian lad was brought out in public a little more than the others used to be. Mary continued to look dolefully at Bernard. Bernard did his best to avoid her. He went to all the girls' gigs, and studiously talked to Lela and Sharkey when not talking to Mop. He began to take a really active interest in the band, and would make occasional comments about the sound mix not being quite right and suggest a new graphic designer for the band's artwork. Mary found his "helpful comments" hugely irritating, and bit her lip to avoid roaring at him. Mop became more and more besotted with Bernard. She talked about him all the time. The others said that she had become a Bernard bore. She never stayed out late with the girls any longer, but went home early with Bernard. Mary, Lela and Sharkey frequently sat up watching videos in Mary's flat, and the hole in their company made them feel as though one of them had died. Lela couldn't manage to tie Mop down for appointments to work on songs. Mop kept cancelling. Her mind was no longer on the band.

Mary decided to call a meeting to talk to Mop about the problem. Mary, Lela and Sharkey were sitting in Mary's flat, waiting for Mop to come, when she phoned and cancelled.

"This is the last straw," said Mary. "She has obviously totally lost interest, she can't even be bothered to come to a meeting."

"Hold on," said Sharkey, "What has Mop done wrong? It's inevitable that she'd start shagging somebody. Mary, you couldn't expect to keep her as an acolyte for ever. Or did you expect that? She's gone, so you don't have your slave. You're forced to bring Brian home with you occasionally. Well, that's just tough. But it wasn't fair of you to try and keep her, because you were giving her nothing. You just gobbled up her affections but gave her nothing."

"And since when did you become a bleedin' psychiatrist?" said Mary.

"I have spent enough time in psychiatric hospitals to have a degree in psychiatry. I am the genuine article psychiatric graduate. The Bachelor of the looney bin. I watch, Mary. You have decided that I'm a flake, because that suits your world view, you can box me and control me. And you're right to an extent, but when I drift off into my own world, I think about things. OK. Mop has cancelled the meeting, and that's out of line. But, I will not

126

let you take out your personal grievance on her.
You're just sour because she left you for Mr
Bailey's Irish Cream. Well, if you couldn't see that
that was bound to happen, then you've less brains
than I thought."

"What on earth are you talking about, Sharkey?
What do you mean 'she left me for Mr Bailey's Irish
Cream'. The way you're going on, you'd swear
we'd been lovers."

"You have a very simplistic view of love."

Mary had never seen Sharkey like this before.
Sharkey, who always drifted around in a daze, was
now being astoundingly logical.

Lela had no opinion about anything. She felt
that everything was fine, and there was no need to
stir trouble with Mop. She didn't mind having
songwriting meetings cancelled, wasn't it a small
price to pay to see Mop with a smile on her face.
Besides, cancelled meetings could always be
rearranged. And she felt that they'd been going for
three years, and had got stuck in a rut. Of course it
wasn't going to remain the same for ever.

"But you guys don't understand. I've worn my
fingers to the bone getting this band on the road.
I've given it everything. I've sacrificed everything
for it. Nothing is going to interfere with it at this
stage. We're on the verge of making it big. We
need all hands on deck. All energies behind the
work."

"Well, if you feel it's necessary, talk to her," said
Lela.

Mary phoned Mop the next day. Bernard always

answered the phone. She and he exchanged barbed chit chat. Mary wished that just for once she could phone Mop and not have to listen to Bernard's inane pleasantries.

"How are you, Mary?"

"Not so bad, and you?"

"Fine, fine. Anything strange?"

"Hmmmnn, nothing too strange. Reported any interesting news lately?"

"This and that."

"Is Mop there?"

"I'll get her for you now." And Bernard went off to fetch the prisoner. Mop sounded almost drugged these days. She sounded as if she was just out of bed, or just about to get into it. Mary arranged to meet her the next day. Mop was delighted. She hadn't seen Mary for a while, and was looking forward to it. She was so blissed out on lurve that she hadn't the least suspicion what she was in for.

The following morning, Mary turned over the situation in her head. She gathered all her evidence, the broken appointments, the unreliabilities, the lack of driving energy. She paced up and down the flat, sharpening her guillotine, until Mop arrived. Mary hadn't seen her for a while outside of the actual sessions in Maguires. Hadn't seen her in daylight. Mop looked lovely. She had dropped a bit of weight, and her skin was clearer.

"Hi Babes, how are ya, give us a kiss," said Mop and threw her arms round Mary. "I haven't seen you in ages, we need to spend some more time together." She grinned vacantly at Mary.

Mary thought that Mop's IQ had halved since she started seeing Bernard. Mop used to be bright as a button, never missed a trick. Now she seemed to have no peripheral vision. She was a bit sad. And the awful thing was that she had no idea how sad she was. Mop was under some kind of illusion that her life was better since she'd met Bernard, but Mary knew that this was not so. Mop had no idea how silly she'd become. She giggled all the time, said nothing of interest, gazed adoringly at Mr Armani Jackets as though she expected him to sprout wings.

"So how are you, Mares?" said Mop, unconcernedly, not really asking a question at all.

Mary wanted to list Mop's offences and unreliabilities, but somehow all that came out was:

"It's Bernard. He bugs the hell out of me."

"I know," said Mop. "But what can I do about that? He is my lover. What is it you want me to do? Ditch him?"

"No, of course not. Just leave him at home once in a while, and try and get three sentences out without mentioning his name. And the band is suffering. You keep missing appointments, standing up Lela, and the rest of us."

"Mary, I do not have to take this bullshit from you. You may get to push us all around in the band, but you're not going to push me around in my personal life. You should be delighted that I've found somebody who's making me happy."

"Happy. Huh. You're not happy. You're going round in a daze like an eejit."

"Mary, I do think it's fair to say that I would be more expert on that matter than you."

"I'm sorry. This isn't coming out right. It's just that with Bernard around, you don't seem to be giving enough time to the band."

"Mary, you're overreacting to him. Did you think I was going to remain a nun in the convent of Lizzards forever? Just look at the situation calmly. There is an inevitability to it. You see, Bernard is Yoko Ono."

"What do you mean Bernard is Yoko Ono?"

"Well, John Lennon and Paul McCartney were . . ."

Something Formal

A swish gathering in the Westbury Hotel. John Quinn was being presented as a full partner in the firm. The entire company was there, and the Chairman. Everybody had their husbands or wives with them, and good wines and fishy nibblies were served. John Quinn felt good. It had been a good year. He had got a lot of work done. And he had just got engaged to a delightful woman whom he had met eight months previously. Everything in life was just right. Claudia, his fiancee, was a theatre set designer, and was working on something big at the moment, so she said she'd be a little late, but she wouldn't miss it. Still, she hadn't arrived yet. John Quinn talked to everybody, and felt very lively. He was having a glass of wine too many, he knew, but what the hell. He chatted away to Mrs Collins, the wife of Joseph A Collins, the man who had taken him into the firm, and to whom he was chiefly indebted for the success he was celebrating today. She was a nice woman, very friendly, and very charming. He was a frequent dinner guest at her house, and he liked both her and her husband very much. In mid conversation, Mrs Collins suddenly said:

"There's a girl over there in the scruffiest denim jacket I've ever seen. It's all holes and it's covered in paint. And she has the filthiest pair of dungarees on. I don't know where she thinks she is, but, honestly, young people have no sense of decorum nowadays. I mean, this is obviously not a lounge bar. It is clearly an occasion for a certain degree of formality. I even think she has some dirt on her face."

John didn't need to turn around. He knew that Claudia would be looking scruffy, she always looked scruffy, unless she was dressed up, and then she looked strange. He turned to look, and across the room her saw her, a vision in denim and paint splatters, her long fuzzy red hair tied back with a blue and white striped sock. Claudia waved at him and called across the room "Hi Babes!", and then continued her conversation with Mrs Doolin, the wife of the Chairman. Claudia was very easy in company, and could talk to almost anyone. It didn't seem to dawn on her that she looked out of place.

John turned back to Mrs Collins and said "That's my fiancee." Mrs Collins, being exceedingly well bred, did not like to offend. She considered her own social boo-boo as bad as Claudia's dress sense, and immediately turned a few spectacular conversational cartwheels. "Well, I suppose I'm just terribly old-fashioned. I have these notions of formality that have probably gone out with the ark.

She is a rather pretty girl, I must say. I'm always telling our Ciara that she dresses a bit conservatively. She dresses like somebody middle aged, she should enjoy her youth." John appreciated Mrs Collins's cartwheels. He watched as Claudia's blue and white striped sock worked the crowd. She was a breath of fresh air in this mausoleum of suits. Claudia finally made her way to his side.

"Sorry I'm so late. I was painting like a dervish to get everything finished." He could see she had black paint on her nose.

That night, as he lay in bed beside her, spent, he thought about Mrs Collins. He wondered should he tell Claudia about her remarks, but decided against it. It would only make her self-conscious. He thought about Claudia's other clothes. They had always seemed quite nice to him, very sexy. She had these flowy blouses and coloured long skirts. She wore loose clothes that looked as if they might fall off her at any minute. There was something inherently wanton about her appearance. He got up and went for a piss, he knew he was going to have a night of insomnia. Once the light was on, he looked around, first at the sleeping Claudia, then at the rest of the room. It had originally been his flat, and she'd moved in with him. Her clothes lay about the room in piles, one pile for every day of the week. She just stepped out of her clothes, let them stay where they fell, slept naked, and plucked new ones from the hot press the next day. He picked them all up every Saturday, separated them into whites and coloureds, and brought them to the launderette. This was a procedure she never commented upon. She never asked how the clothes appeared miraculously in the hot press. He wondered if she knew that she had thirty-one pairs of knickers? When he'd counted them, he thought the figure significant. It meant she could survive a month with clean knickers. He hung up his clothes every night.

Her clothes never saw an iron. She wore them all wrinkly, and never seemed to notice that they looked odd. And now that he thought about it, she never did any housework. She just left her plate on the table, and expected it to be taken away and washed and put back in the press. When she buttered her toast in the morning, she didn't put all the butter from the knife onto the toast, but scooped the knife, still buttery, into the marmalade, scraped a little of the marmalade onto the toast, and left the knife, covered in both butter and marmalade, down flat on the table. She didn't know what a mess this made because she never wiped the table. Her mother must have spoiled her, he concluded. He knew enough about her background to know that she certainly wasn't used to maids. It was a small thing, of course, what were a few dirty plates, and a bit of buttery marmalade, in the context of the greatest passion he had ever dreamed of?

And, on the positive side, she was very handy. She could make a bed. Not in the sense of sheets and pillow cases, she never did that, but literally make it. He had bought a new double bed to celebrate her arrival into his flat, but the magnificent oak bed had arrived in do-it-yourself assembly bits. He was gob-smacked, and was about to phone the store to complain, but she just got out a screwdriver, and started screwing.

He watched her as she slept, dreaming and unconscious of the bad thoughts that were creeping into his head. Maybe he should loosen up. Maybe it didn't matter if there were bundles of clothes all over the floor of the bedroom, and dirty knives in the kitchen. She was a joy to him. He cuddled up beside her, and fell asleep.

Two days later, John received an invitation from Mrs Collins for himself and Claudia to come to dinner in a fortnight's time. It was obviously Mrs Collins's way of making up for her inadvertent rudeness. John checked with Claudia, and then accepted. It was for a Friday night. He began to worry about Claudia. He loved her, but if she was going to be his wife, then she'd have to start considering how she would fit into his workplace. He thought of all his colleagues' wives, they all looked very well groomed. Some of them had daughters who looked like Claudia – at college and so on – but not wives. On the Thursday night before the Friday they were due at the Collins's, John brought his credit card into town to do some late night shopping. He went to the ladies department of Brown Thomas, and picked out a pale blue jacket and skirt. It was a little box jacket, and a tight skirt, which fell to just above the knee.

One of the sales assistants, whom he judged to be about Claudia's size, modelled it for him. John explained what he wanted; he said it was a present for his fiancee, and he wanted something nice and formal, but at the same time reflecting her sparkiness and creativity. The sales assistant recommended the suit, but said that it was a little old-fashioned and she picked out a cream sparkly blouse, which was low cut; this added a certain snazziness to the overall effect, while still being classy. He got the whole lot packed up in a box and brought it home.

Claudia was delighted to receive a present, and fell on the box. She opened it up and took out the contents. He studied her face as she looked at the garments.

"I thought you'd like to have something formal."

She tried on the clothes, leaving the ones she'd been wearing in a heap on the floor, and walked around the living-room. John had thought that the outfit would really suit her lean, greyhound-like figure, but it made her look odd. It was fine when she stood still, but when she moved, she looked . . . He couldn't exactly figure out what was wrong with how she looked.

"I feel like I'm in drag," she said, and giggled.

That was it. That was exactly it. She looked as if she was wearing clothes designed for a different gender. He wasn't sure from her face whether or not she got the subtext of his gift. He suspected that she did. She was very smart, especially in matters of subtext.

The following night, without having to be told, Claudia put on the blue suit. She also put her hair up on top of her head in clips. John couldn't help feeling guilty. He felt he'd deceived and betrayed her. She was obviously awkward in the outfit. It was much tighter-fitting than she was used to. The cut of the shoulders required that she stand up straight and poke out her chest, and the low cut blouse exposed quite a lot of her cleavage. The tightness and shortness of the skirt meant that she had to sit with her knees together. It looked so wrong on her, he couldn't understand why she had agreed to wear it. He wanted to tell her to take it off, but he felt that this would only compound his sin.

"Do you like it?" he asked.

"Yes, it's very nice," she replied. He couldn't figure out if she was saying this because he had given it to her as a present, or did she really think it? He knew that he had made a mess of things, but wasn't quite sure how to put it right. It was with some trepidation that he set out for the night with Claudia on his arm.

Things went very well in the Collinses' house to begin with. They all stood around the drawing-room for a while, sipping drinks. Present were Dermot Coyle, also a partner in the firm, and his wife Jane, who used to work in the accounts department, but had left to rear their family. Also the Johnsons, whom John had met before and were old friends of the Collinses. Charlie Johnson had roomed with Joseph Collins when they were in

college, and that was a long time ago. His wife,
Annemarie, was younger than him, and very chic.
She looked mid-thirties, but he knew her to be
forty-five. He watched Claudia. She did look
stunning. The powder blue suit really showed off
the violent colour of her hair, which looked lovely
piled up on her head. He was proud of her, she
would pass the most stringent Mrs Collins test. And
she still seemed to be easy and chatty with
everybody. They went into the dining-room. John
was placed beside Joseph Collins, Claudia beside
Mrs Collins. He would have rathered they sat
together. John only semi-engaged with the
conversation at his end of the table and kept an ear
out for what was going on at the other end. Mrs
Collins was being very friendly.

"The theatre is a lovely career. I always say to
Joe that our kids are overly influenced by him
being so successful. They've all gone into
traditional businesses. I would've liked one of them
to do something creative. But, I suppose, children
never please their mother."

"Yes, my mother wanted me to go into the civil
service. She kept sending me for exams. She has
no time for the instability of the freelancer's life."

"The lovely aspect to the freelance thing,
especially for a girl, is that you can easily take time
off to have a baby." She winked at her. "It's a
terrible thing when you have to choose between
motherhood and a career."

"Oh, I don't think there's any danger of that, for
the immediate future. I did seriously consider

having a baby last year, because I was pregnant.
Nothing makes you consider having a baby like
being pregnant. But I didn't feel it was right for me
at the time, so I had an abortion."

John choked on his soup. Soup is a very
difficult thing to choke on, but he managed it. Mrs
Collins was shocked, but almost managed to
conceal it.

"Oh my dear, I'm very sorry to hear that. Was it
John's?"

"No, it was before John. Actually, I was mainly
with a female lover at the time, but the pregnancy
was the result of a one night stand with another old
flame of mine. Jacintha, my girlfriend, was delighted.
She went around town claiming that she was the only
lesbian on earth who had impregnated her mot."

John finished a huge glass of wine in one gulp.

"So, are you a l-l-lesbian?" Mrs Collins asked,
almost unable to speak.

"Sometimes. I don't believe that sexuality is as
easily boxed as society likes to think. I think a lot
of people would be happier with a member of the
same sex. It is only because we are conditioned by
fairy stories about princes and princesses from a
very early age that we don't consider it."

At this stage, all the guests were listening to the
conversation at Claudia's end of the table. John
opened his top button and loosened his tie.

"For instance," said Claudia, in full flight now,
"most people can masturbate to orgasm themselves,
and most people could masturbate somebody else
to orgasm. So the technicalities are not a problem."

"Excuse me, while I clear the soup plates," said Mrs Collins. She cleared the table, and went out to the kitchen to find the main dish.

"Lovely soup," said Claudia.

"But what about the romance?" asked Jane Coyle, Dermot Coyle's wife.

"Yeah," said Dermot, "what about the romance?"

"Well," replied Claudia, "let's break romance down into its component parts-"

"Component parts, it's not a motorcycle," said Dermot.

"Well in many ways it is like a motorcycle," said Claudia. "There are many disparate elements, which, when they're all put together in a particular way, work very well to transport somebody from A to B."

"I agree with her," said Jane, "You have to be able to break down love, because otherwise we'd all be saying 'I love him because I love him' and that's silly. I can tell you, point for point, why Dermot thrills me. I can also tell you what bugs me about him. So if you subtract the bugs from the thrills, and you evaluate what's left, then you know if you have love or not."

"You can take the woman out of the accountancy office, but you can't take the calculator out of the woman," said Dermot.

"I can see the ladies are joining forces against us," said Joseph Collins, and winked at John.

Mrs Collins came in with a joint of roast lamb, and her teenage daughter Aileen followed with a dish of roast potatoes. Aileen, like a particularly well-trained waitress, dished out the potatoes onto each hot plate, and brought vegetables forth from the hostess trolley.

"Well," said Claudia, "for the sake of argument, let's say that romance is made up of compatability, mutual interest, and sexual attraction. Sexual attraction usually means that you consider the other person to be beautiful. Now, I consider you to be quite beautiful, Jane, and I could easily find you sexually attractive if-"

"Mint sauce, Claudia?" said Mrs Collins.

"Ah, thank you," said Claudia.

"Perhaps we'll leave the conversation on hold for a while until we have the dinner served up," said Mrs Collins. "Fascinating though it is."

This silenced Claudia.

John spoke. "What a delicious looking roast. Mmmmh! And those potatoes look divine!"

"Bravo Mary," said Joseph.

There was an awkward silence until Aileen left the room.

"I just thought the conversation was a little adult for Aileen. She is only sixteen. Sorry to have silenced you."

"I'm sorry," said Claudia, and she gave a little apologetic, embarrassed laugh, "but when I was sixteen, at boarding school, we used to have competitions in the showers to see who could come first with the aid of the shower nozzles. I'm sure Aileen has much racier conversations than we're having now. At that age, the only thing you are interested in is sex."

Mrs Collins fanned herself with her napkin. John knew she wanted to shut Claudia up, but couldn't bring herself to be rude. John tried to think of something totally unrelated to say, but his mind was blank.

"Delicious lamb, this is truly delicious," was all he managed. Charlie and Annemarie Johnson, who had both been silent up to now, both started to speak at the same time.

"Sorry darling, you go ahead."

"No you do."

"Well, I was just going to say that the lamb is delicious."

"Ah. I was admiring the broccoli."

"What I want to know is, under what circumstances would you find me sexually attractive?" asked Jane Coyle of Claudia. "You said a minute ago you'd find me attractive if? If what? That's what I want to know."

"Yeah, I'd like to know that as well," said her husband Dermot.

"I'd be interested too," said John.

"Would you consider it?" said Claudia, with the boldest of faces, and a very lively wicked eyebrow raised to Jane, and it was then that John realised that she was taking revenge for the outfit. He realised, by that one raised eyebrow, that Claudia was raging about how she had been turned out, and was punishing him for it. Her eyes were glistening now, from drink and merriment. They assumed a mad sparkle. Some of her hair had started to fall down, and seated as she was, there was a lot of cleavage showing. He wished he'd bought her a slightly more decent blouse. No he didn't. He loved her more than ever at that moment. He started to have an erection.

Jane Coyle was well able to give as good as she got. "I might," she said.

"You would not," said her husband, in a narked tone.

"Loosen up, Dermy," she said.

"Well, maybe we'll meet up for a drink sometime, and explore the if?" said Claudia.

Mrs Collins was a little tipsy, having taken refuge from her dinner guests in her wine glass, and suddenly started to find the scenario amusing. "Lord above," she said, "we've never had a dinner party before where somebody's fiancee started to seduce somebody's wife. This is a scream," and she gave a mad hysterical laugh.

Joseph Collins stared at her in astonishment.

John had never heard Mrs Collins laugh before. In all the years he'd known her, he had never heard anything like the mirth that was shaking her frame. "An absolute scream," and she roared laughing again. The laughter was infectious, and everybody joined in, hysterically, everybody except Dermot Coyle.

"Shall I clear the plates?" asked Aileen, who appeared round the door with a smirk. She had obviously been listening to everything outside in the hall.

"Thank you, darling," said Mrs Collins, "Yes now, who's for dessert, or rather, what's for dessert?" and she went into peals of laughter again at her mistake.

That night, when they got home, John knew better than to take Claudia to task for talking about her lesbianisms and her abortions in so public a way. They were both quite woozy from the wine. Claudia went into the bedroom first, and by the time he joined her, the powder blue suit was in a pile on the floor, just like the seven other piles, one from earlier today when she'd changed into the suit, and six others from the six days since last Saturday's laundry. Claudia was in the bed, either asleep, or pretending. He picked up her blue suit, put it on a hanger, and into the wardrobe. It would be ruined by a night on the floor. And then, he took off his clothes, hung them up, and got in beside her.

Wedding Bells

When we came out of the registry office, I noticed a woman in the waiting-room who looked very familiar.

"Orla Browne?" she asked tentatively.

"Geraldine Masterson!" I replied.

She was an old school friend of mine. I hadn't seen her in seven years. Literally seven years. "Gosh! What are you doing here?"

"Well. Isn't it obvious? Alan, this is Orla, an old school friend."

Alan smiled and shook my hand, he looked sweet, he had a good-natured chin. I introduced them to Kevin, my intended.

I laughed. "Geraldine, do you remember Sister Mary Skipping Rope, our PE teacher who used to make us recite the Apostle's Creed and if we fluffed, she shook her cane and told us that the last girl she taught who didn't know the twelve articles of the Apostles' Creed had come to a terrible end, she married an atheist in a registry office."

"Oh yes! I remember that." She laughed. "I always knew it off by heart, and so did you. In fact you were a total swot, if I remember correctly."

"And here we are, marrying atheists in a registry office." I giggled and called goodbye and good luck as Kevin and I dashed out the door and dodged raindrops on the way to Bewley's. We had just lodged our application to get married with the registrar, an eccentric grey woman with flaking hair who smoked two cigarettes at once, one strategically placed by the phone and the other by the filing cabinet.

Kevin's dad died when he was eight. His mother is a very proper woman. We called there with our news, and she opened a bottle of champagne. I could tell that she wasn't completely ecstatic about the match. Mrs Kavanagh had somebody more sophisticated in mind for her son, Princess Caroline of Monaco, for instance. Kevin has always protected her from me. He says that he loves me dearly, but life will be much simpler for us if I keep my views on certain things to myself in the company of his family. Also I'm not allowed to say "fuck" when I'm with them. He tried to persuade me to take out my nose stud when I go there, but I drew the line at that. I know that he also cautions them. He makes his mother promise not to make pointed remarks about propriety of dress in my company.

"So, who's your parish priest, Orla?" asked Mrs Kavanagh.

"Pardon?" I replied.

"Your parish priest, who'll do the ceremony, dear. I presume it'll be in your parish."

"Well, we're not getting married in a church.

We're getting married in the registry office." Kevin had said that, if we could manage it, we'd not mention this detail at this stage. But what could I do? I was asked a straight question, I couldn't lie. For a moment, I thought Mrs Kavanagh was going to faint. She sat down on her chair.

"What?" she gasped.

"You heard her," said Kevin bravely, though I could hear a slight waver in his voice. His mother was the one person who could get at him.

"But you can't."

"We can, and we are going to," he said.

"But what about the rest of the family? What will they think?"

"Mother, I'm not getting married for the rest of the family, I'm getting married for myself, and Orla of course."

"It's your self I'm talking about. You may be pleasuring the flesh here on earth, but what about your immortal soul?"

"I think I know my immortal soul better than you, Mother."

"No you don't, I gave you life, I reared you. When the day of judgement comes, and you are asked by St Peter why your soul is black, you say you swapped it for the earthly bauble of sexual pleasure."

Kevin had gone a little white and he stood up. I doubted that he'd ever heard his mother say "sexual pleasure" before.

"Come on Orla, let's go. I don't mind listening to this, but I'm not going to subject you to it.

Mother, you must know that I haven't been to Mass for years and years now."

"I know, but everybody goes through that phase. But then, when they get married, they return to the church. Your brother and sisters have done it. I know they didn't go to Mass when they lived in England, but they still got married in church, and they started going once their children arrived. I know young people of twenty can't be bothered with religion for a while. They have to go through their rebellion phase, Orla, what do you think? You were reared a Catholic, weren't you?"

"Yes, but I grew up a feminist."

"A feminist. Huh! Baby butcherers. Well, let me tell you both now, not only will I not come to this affair, but neither of you need darken my door if you go ahead with this travesty. What will I say to everybody? My son and his harlot in a registry office."

"Well, I'm sorry you feel like that, Mother. Goodbye." Kevin was about to go, but decided to make one last-ditch attempt.

"Mother, surely what we want and what will make us happy is the important thing."

"Don't talk to me about happiness, you know nothing about happiness. All ye know about is pleasure."

We walked out into the rain and sat in the car. I couldn't help feeling annoyed with Kevin. He attempted all the time to smooth over things, to deny things, and he was reaping the rewards of this now. And he had got me caught up in his game. Kevin had never told his mother we were living together. Since I moved in with him, I have never been allowed to answer the phone before midday, because it would indicate that I've stayed overnight. All my stuff is kept in the spare room in his flat, to make it look as if I sleep there if I stay over. He has a good heart, and his motivation is very pure, but he will have to face the fact that he can't please all the people all the time. He has to establish a hierarchy of pleasee's. And in my book his mother was a bit too high up in this hierarchy.

We called to my parents' house a little more tentatively than we did to his. Somehow, I found it excrutciating and mortifying. I have always found weddings comical and embarrassing. My mother nearly fainted with joy. She had long ago given up hope of shifting me. She found my sartorial negligence appalling, especially since I bought the bovver boots, and got the hair chopped. She wondered how any man might ever look at me, let alone take me seriously. My mother wondered what on earth Kevin saw in me. He seemed to be such a regular nice guy kind of chap, but she was glad of it nonetheless. Straight up, I told them about the registry office.

My mother didn't give a tosser, delighted as she is to get me married off, she wouldn't care if I did it in an abattoir. My father, however, had a soft spot for his only girl.

"What!" he exclaimed. "But only atheists get married there."

"Well, we are atheists."

"Nonsense Girlie, you're RC to the bone."

"But we're not. Neither of us have practised religion for years."

"This family has been Catholic for generations. Your grandfather kept the watches of the night while Saorstát Éireann was a-borning. For generations this family has fought to get the Brits off this island so we could practise our faith in peace and dignity. Don't tell me you haven't been to Mass for years. Your flesh and blood have been going to Mass for a thousand years. It's in your bones, Girlie. What's a few years of your life when it's pitched against thousands of years of a glorious tradition? People have lost their lives in order that you have the freedom to practise your religion. I don't give you permission."

"But Dada, it's 1995, I don't need your permission. Women have the vote now, remember."

"More wine anybody?" my mother asked. She has this way of absolutely not noticing what she doesn't wish to notice. It's a great trick.

"Kevin, you're a sensible young man. You're a Catholic, aren't you? Talk her out of this. My daughter's always been difficult, that bloody convent she went to didn't do her any good at all, those damn nuns were always subversive."

"Mr Browne, I'm not a Catholic."

"But your parents are."

"Yes, but I'm not."

"What are you then?"

"I'm an agnostic."

"Oh, nonsense. You are not, you're a Catholic.

You sound like one. You look like one. I can spot a non-Catholic at forty paces. The Kavanaghs were always Catholics. Good Cork name, Kavanagh."

"That's a lovely tweed suit, Kevin," said my mother, sweetly.

I began to lose my temper. "Dad, we are not here to seek either your permission or your approval, we are simply informing you of our decision to get married."

"All of your brothers got married in church."

I have seven older brothers, all of whom were married by the age of twenty-three. My mother spoiled them so much that they all grew up idiotic and married replicas of her as fast as they could.

"I know, but look at them. Two of them are separated. Three of them are in serious difficulties. It's hardly an example."

"Well, that's the bottom line. I don't give you permission."

"Dad, we don't need your permission."

"Whether you need it or not, you're not getting it."

"Would anybody like some cheese and crackers?" my mother asked.

We left and went out into the rainy night.

"I told you it'd be difficult," said Kevin.

"Yep, they were awful. But they're always awful about everything."

"Orla, you have to see their point. They think that they've failed in their religious duty to rear us as Catholics, and that's a big thing for them. They are, as and from tonight, religious failures."

151

"I don't give a damn. They're a disgrace, and I'm cutting them off."

"You can't be so absolute, Orla, they're entitled to their view."

"No they are not. They can all buzz off. If they think that they're going to bully me up a fuckin' aisle and into a white dress, they must be bonkers."

"Well, we could consider it, for the sake of peace. We don't need a white dress and an aisle, we could go to a little side chapel somewhere and I could wear a white dress."

Kevin, though I love him dearly, is too willing to negotiate. It probably comes from being a Libran. He just loves compromises. It makes him feel as if he's experiencing a triumph of reason. He should have been a diplomat. He's great at making concessions, even concessions to idiocy. He loves pulling over to let ambulances pass because it makes him feel as if he's a member of a functioning civilisation. My birth sign is Taurus and I am a bull. I am, by nature, completely resolute. My mother was so busy spoiling my brothers, I learned independence at an early age. If I hadn't fought for it, I would have never been given steak for dinner. I was never encouraged at school, because too much education would make me into a bad wife. My mother instructed me in all the ways of the kitchen, while my brothers grew up thinking that tea was delivered sugared and stirred. Third level education was seen as a waste of money for me, because I'd give it all up and have babies. The birth accident of my gender rendered me compromised to such an extent that I refused to compromise on any other issue. I only barely accepted my girlness, and never wore dresses.

Kevin knows that I am like a harridan when I feel violated, so he had the wisdom not to push the point any further.

The following day we received phone calls from all our combined brothers and sisters, ten in all, telling us how we were breaking our mothers' hearts. "Don't be ridiculous, my mother doesn't have a heart," I said, "she has a statue of the Infant of Prague instead. And your mother doesn't have a heart either." Kevin said that I was becoming unreasonable and that I couldn't blame them for what they were like. And, after all, they did give birth to us and bring us up.

"I know," I said, "but it wasn't because they loved us, it was because their stupid religion doesn't allow for contraception." Kevin said that I was definitely unreasonable now, and I said, "Maybe you'd better find yourself someone more fuckin' reasonable for a wife then." That was just before I banged the door and walked out.

It was only when I was on the street that I realised that I had nowhere to go. I had given up my flat when I moved in with Kevin, and Ciara, my ex-flatmate, had moved her boyfriend Patrick into the space I vacated. I went and sat in the park for a while, watched the ducks, and contemplated becoming a tramp. There were three tramps who always sat on a particular bench there, slugging cans of Scrumpy Jack cider. They always looked happy, as did the ducks. They lived without rules and regulations, they did what came naturally, according to their duck instincts and their tramp instincts.

When I arrived at Ciara's house, Kevin had got there before me. He was sitting at the kitchen table, happily lapping up tea and sympathy from Ciara and Patrick. All my friends like Kevin better than they like me. My friends tend to see me as a problem to be solved. "Poor Orla" they say. Everybody likes Kevin because he's so bloody nice. I suppose that's why I like him too. He has this way of getting people on his side. I, apparently, have this way of alienating everybody. Kevin was in a state and begged me to come home.

"Well, what are we going to do about our problem?" I asked.

"It's not our problem, it's everybody else's problem. Let them sort it out."

So I went back home with him. But, there were going to be some changes. Firstly, it was going to be made clear to everybody that we were living together. All ambiguity relating to this topic was to be removed. Secondly, his mother's habit of just dropping by, unannounced, was to stop. My father called his solicitor and re-wrote his will, cutting me out of it. He sent me a copy. I sent him a copy of my application to have my name changed to Orla Starship Enterprise, my family name having been disgraced by his dinosaur attitudes. Kevin's mother started sending us religious literature anonymously. So I sent her material on witchcraft and Wicca, also anonymously, and some quiche recipes, just for devilment. Kevin said that this was childish. I told him to tell his mother that she was childish too. He said this was even more childish. My parents and his mother ganged up and had pan-parent meetings. Family conferences were called. Novenas were said. Delegations of my brothers were sent to reason with me, and were unceremoniously booted out the door. When this failed, legions of my sisters-in-law were sent, waving their babies like crucifixes. Kevin's mother refused to speak to him when he called her. She wept and kept saying that he and his harlot had broken his mother's heart. I said that if his mother referred to me one more time as a "harlot" I was going to break her windows, never mind her heart. She went on a retreat and appointed Kevin's sister Marian as her representative on earth. Marian hounded Kevin, by day and by night.

I didn't mind the rows with my family. I was used to battles. I was a warrior. They all gave me the pip anyway. But I could see the toll it took on Kevin. He was very close to his family, and he couldn't bear being cut off from them. The fact that he was right was no comfort to him. He looked miserable all the time, the joy had gone out of him. He had constructed his life full of deceits designed to make everybody happy in their ignorance. I had forced him to rearrange his life according to truths, which made everybody miserable.

Weeks passed, and our wedding day drew closer. I was determined to go through with it.

Kevin stopped sleeping and eating. He started having nightmares. We argued all the time. We were the most miserable nearly-weds you could imagine. Yet we ploughed on. I, out of a sense of total bullishness. Nothing like a good and just fight to get me out of the bed in the morning. Kevin's motivation was a little less clear. But he was determined also. When asked about it he said:

"Because fundamentally I believe it to be right. We should have the freedom to do what we want, not what everybody else wants. It's not easy, but it's right."

I really felt for him. For me it was easy. For him it was a terrible struggle. He really valued what he was losing. It was then that I realised that they had won. No matter how much we battled, they had won. They had succeeded in making us miserable, in stealing the pleasure of our marriage.

I went out once more to talk to the ducks. They still looked very happy, just being ducks, giving the occasional quack, and sailing round and round the pond. And the tramps sat there happily slugging their Scrumpy Jack, while I, in full control of an unsozzled human brain, could not find a way round this problem.

I went home to Kevin, and I told him I wanted to call it off. Cancel the wedding. I knew he couldn't cancel it. It was too wrong a thing for him to do. But I could do it. It was a warrior's job to surrender. It was OK for me to do it, because I was doing it for him. Orla Starship Enterprise was hanging up her guns.

At first Kevin misunderstood me. "But Orla, we can't let them do that, let them separate us."

"Who said anything about separating? We'll just stay living together. Announce our engagement or something. Buy some diamond rings. Put an ad in the paper, pick out some white dress recipes. They should be able to handle that."

"But our wedding? We want to get married."

"We can wait, darling. Our revenge on the older generation. We outlive them. We'll have our wedding dance on their graves."

Goo Goo

"Drinnng! drinng!"

Although in mid-egg frying, I lunge for the phone in order to answer it before the machine. Too late. "Hi! You've reached 349 0604, we can't come to the phone right now . . ."

"Hello hello," I say. "Don't mind the machine I'm turning it off." I grab the machine, wrestle it to the ground and finally overpower it.

"Hello. Sorry about that."

"Hi Mags, it's Rachael."

"Hi Ra Ra."

"Mags, how are ya doin?"

"Grand and you?"

"Fine. Except Oisin's sick. He's got a tummy bug so he's awake all night and crying all the time. The poor mite. I think he'll be OK but I'm getting pretty exhausted. I haven't slept in two days. I've finally got him off to sleep now."

"Aw poor thing."

"No, I think he'll be OK."

"I meant you."

"I took him to the doctor, and she said he'll have to weather it out."

"It's his job. He's a baby. Getting sick is his job."

"Ssssh! Ssssh!"

"What?"

"Ssssh!"

"!!??!!"

"I'd better go. I can hear him waking."

And Rachael hangs up. I hang up too and go back to my egg which is now scorched. I can't remember when I last had a decent conversation with Rachael. I never see her without the baby. When she calls to see me she brings three wallets of photos of Oisin, and when she finally coaxes the child to sleep, she takes out the photos and we look at them. She gets a little bit hurt when I say "I think that you didn't quite manage to get Oisin into the very centre of this shot," but she recovers quickly. "Mags, you're nothing if not blunt," she says.

I eat my poor egg, burnt side up.

John, my lover, wants to have a baby. Or to be more exact, he wants me to have a baby. His baby obviously. I tell him not to be so old-fashioned. But I don't know how long I'll be able to hold out. He hasn't quite threatened to leave me if I don't, but I can see it coming. He says that he loves me dearly, but part of his "overall life agenda is the production of progeny." He's a businessman, he can't help talking like that, he really is a very nice guy. He loves having Rachael and Oisin over, he sits for hours and goes "Goo goo" at the baby. Rachael didn't used to like John very much, I think she resented his intrusion on our intimacy but, since the baby was born, and John took such an interest in him, she thinks he's a "smashing guy" and amn't I lucky to have him.

Rachael's views on many things changed when she had the baby. She used to be an active feminist. She used to go on marches and make speeches and agitate and write letters to the paper. Now she says she can't do these things anymore, because there is no one to mind the baby. I've told her that that used to be exactly the point of doing them.

John comes home from work. Exhausted. He has a bunch of flowers and a box of chocolates for me. Unusual. It makes me suspicious. No sooner is he in the door but he is on his knees.

"Will you marry me, Mags?"

"Why?"

"What do you mean why? Because I love you."

"What's wrong with the way we are?" I say, panic rising in my voice.

"Because I want us to be together for ever. And I want us to have children. And I want you to be mine, and I want to be yours."

He takes out a little packet from his pocket and puts it in my hand. "Go on, open it."

"I can't."

"Go on."

I open the packet and inside is a beautiful gold ring with a ruby stone in it.

"It's beautiful," I say, and he slips the ring onto my finger (perfect fit) while I'm off-guard because

I'm a bit dazzled by its beauty. I mean to tell him that I'll have to think about it but at this stage John is nibbling my ear and touching me and everything just goes right out of my mind. He wants to do it right here, on the kitchen floor. I don't mind, but don't think I haven't noticed his new penchant for having sex in unusual places, far away from the bathroom closet where the condoms live. He's taken to wanting to do it in fields, forty miles from the nearest condom. I suppose he thinks that I will eventually weaken and not send him off to get them, or else he thinks he'll whip me up into such a frenzy that I'll get careless. Not me, sunshine. I'll never get *that* frenzied. When I send him off for the condoms he pouts and protests, but I insist. The sex is great, as usual. You really have to hand it to John. He sure can fuck. He can't cook. I cook. But he cleans.

I tell John about the phone call with Ra Ra and how I miss having her to talk to and I ask him what he thinks.

"She seems fine, great, never better."

"But you didn't know her that well before. You only knew the outside of her. It's the inside that's changed."

"Well, it's natural that people change as they get older. Of course having a baby will change her. It completely alters all her relationships to everyone around her."

"I know, but . . ."

"Well, then, maybe you need a new best friend. Or . . ."

"Or what?"

"Or . . . maybe you need a baby."

I should have seen that coming.

I look down at the big ruby on my ring finger. It is very pretty. I never said yes though. But I didn't say no either. I do want to marry him. He's lovely. We suit. I'm just a bit scared. It's mainly the baby thing. I'm trying to develop a siege mentality, because I'm afraid he'll wear me down. I have to be completely alert and on my guard all the time, or he'll get me at a weak moment.

My mother used to work in the bank, before she met my father and got married. She was duly frog-marched by the State out of her job and into the home, where she produced seven of us. On her wedding day, my mother became a slave, a slave to my generation. This did not seem to bother her, but I have never got over it. Yesterday I saw a woman on the bus with a child. The little girl was looking out the window and spotting things she knew the name of. "House house house" and "Tree tree tree" and "Birdee birdee birdee". Her mother smiled at her and said "Yes, clever girl. Yes, clever girl." This lasted all the way into town. It made me think of Rachael. Rachael, that fine intellect, that biting wit, that incisive commentator on current affairs. Oh, I despair.

I invite Rachael over the following Saturday afternoon. She looks terrible. Her hair is greasy and straggly. Her dress is unironed. Oisin is sparkling like a new pin. Rachael rearranges the furniture in my living-room to make a playden for him and scatters his toys everywhere. Lolly, my little dog, is banished to the back garden.

"The dog is dirty," explains Rachael.

"I beg your pardon. The dog is not dirty. The dog is housetrained. Which is more than can be said for your baby, who shits at will, and has to be cleaned up after."

"Have I told you, his poos are getting much more solid now. To begin with, his poos were really runny and greenish, like a curry, but now they're browner and firmer, almost like an adult's. I've started him on solids now. And he only uses four nappies a day. But I'm delighted about the poos. It's great isn't it."

"Fab."

"I've told you about Marina, the woman I met at the mothers and toddlers group, and her little girl Chrissie, only ten months, is actually walking now. She took her first step at the group the other day, she was reaching for Fintan the Fire Engine and she walked. Isn't that amazing? We all clapped."

"Wow."

"Anyway enough about us. How are you? How's business?"

"I'm grand. Business is booming, I can only barely keep up, and I'm charging more and more per job each time and . . ."

The baby starts to waaaa. Rachael picks him up and cuddles him and puts him on her breast, which quietens him.

"Sorry, you were saying?"

"Nothing important."

"He'll go off to sleep now. Oh, I nearly forgot, I must show you the latest photos. They're in my bag. Will you pass it to me?"

I can hear Lolly whining and pawing at the back door.

"Honestly, Rachael, I couldn't bear to wade through another forty photos of Oisin. You only showed me the last batch three weeks ago. He hasn't grown much since then."

"You're right. Sorry. I've become a baby bore."

"Tell me about you. How are you feeling?" I say.

"Mags, you've no idea how happy I am. You know the way I was worried about being tied with the baby and becoming frustrated. Well, it just hasn't happened. I can't bear the thought of leaving him and going back to work, so I'm not going to."

"Ra Ra," I pause and gather my courage. "I find it hard to talk to you now. Our interests are diverging. You're not working any more, so we can't talk about work. You don't go out any more, so we can't talk about plays and films like we used to. You don't go to the women's group anymore, so we can't talk about that and, fond as I am of Oisin, I don't find him endlessly fascinating."

I wait for her to explode in a defensive rage. But she doesn't. She smiles gently and touches my arm.

"It's inevitable, Mags. I have changed. Giving birth *is* a life changing experience." She pauses for a moment. "Why don't *you* have a baby?"

I should have seen that coming too.

I know now why I have been so slow to talk to

her about this. I think I knew the answer all along. She is happy. Blissfully happy. One look at those shining tired eyes. She is ecstatic. Oh God!

John comes home, delighted to find the visitors there. He wakes up the baby to play with him.

"Goo goo," says John.

"Gurgle," says the baby.

The three of them go out for a walk and I settle down and do my accounts. They were supposed to be in on Friday, which was yesterday. In my life, everything is always supposed to have been done yesterday. My business, my lovely business. Maybe my work is as boring to other people as their babies are to me.

John returns. His testosterone has been charged by playing with Oisin in the park. He literally dives on me. We go up to the bedroom and make love. He has a lovely body, tall and hairy and soft. He has lovely gentle hands. Before we start I get the condoms from the bathroom. As we gain motion, I relax and lovely shudders run through me.

"Mags, let me enter you without one. I promise I won't come," he whispers.

"OK," I say, "but just for a minute."

He does so and I feel him come in. It's the thin end of the wedge. It is a different sensation. I find it exciting. I stop thinking. Thought leaves me.

"Can I come inside you, Mags?"

"Yes," I say.

I come too. We both come.

A Perm

Marianne was getting through life just fine. She had herself completely under control. But I suppose it was inevitable that she would lose her grip and do something odd. Something totally unforeseen. This happened last Monday. But before I tell you about it, let me tell you about her.

Marianne is thirty. She lives with her daughter and her partner (neither her husband nor Sheila's father) in a flat near enough to the centre of town. They are reasonably well-off. Paschal, the man who is neither her husband nor the father of her child, works in the antiques business. Marianne works as a voice instructor in a drama school. A fair proportion of Paschal's income goes to support his ex-wife who is rearing his two children in Malahide. Marianne receives nothing from her ex-husband, who disappeared, vanished in a puff of blue smoke, from his cigar. So, they manage, this domestic unit. Their lives are complicated, but happy-ish. Marianne is a tall, lean woman, with long sandy hair, which she wears down her back in a long plait. Her girlfriends, when she used to have them, always thought that this was a terrible waste. She is never seen outdoors with her hair out, but she occasionally lets it down in her home, especially in her bedroom, especially in bed. She likes the feeling of the hair on her clean skin at night. She likes getting Paschal tangled in the hair, as she had previously liked getting his predecessor tangled. But her hair is uncompromising, like iron, and the tangles fall out in the morning. Her hair happily complies with the instructions from the comb, and submits to the plait obediently.

In her classroom, Marianne is formidable. The students are all frightened of her. She never smiles, and can be very cutting. They respect her, work hard for her, never arrive late, but never warm to her. Marianne is happy with this state of affairs. Introduced early to responsibility, she developed a personality able for that responsibility. She has a fierce eye, and sometimes frightens even Paschal. She rarely smiles, rarely appears happy, not even with her daughter. This is not because she is miserable, but rather because it is the way she is. She is not demonstrative, she doesn't cry, she doesn't laugh. She is very practical, she copes.

It is a miracle how Marianne and Paschal found each other. He is terribly terribly shy and full of self-doubt. What buds of self-confidence he did possess in his youth were eradicated by his early marriage to a domineering woman who quickly realised she despised him. When he met Marianne, there was an eerie inevitability to their union. It was as if something beyond themselves took over the situation and looked after them. When they found themselves in each other's arms, they were both astonished, and fucked to get over the embarrassment. But that unspoken pact between them during the night changed them both forever. Chipped a little at their defences, weakened them both enough, created a gap in their patterns, just wide enough to let the other slip through.

Where Marianne had a fierce and formidable appearance, Paschal had a droopy one. There was something sad and down-turned about him. He wore a moustache which curled downwards at the ends. His shoulders bent over slightly, and he had the kind of stature which couldn't wear a suit. It just didn't look right on him, didn't hang right. He seemed ill-fitting, no matter what he did. Before he went out the door, he frequently made an attempt to stand up straight, but it made his stature go from sloppy to awkward, so he usually resumed his slouch before he left. He suspected that this was why his wife had left him. He didn't fit in with her social ambitions. She had taken him to the best tailors in Dublin, but there was nothing they could do for him. He was sartorially incurable. This did not bother Marianne. She was not somebody who rated a man's ability to wear a suit. She herself dressed very practically, dressed as she felt the mother of her daughter should dress.

Sheila, the ten-year-old other element in the household, had acquired the sobriety of her mother at an early age. She was not unhappy, just quiet and practical. She was unexcitable, and observant. Other children thought her unfriendly, and adults thought her oddly mature. She looked at everything as though she was logging it in some mental notebook, and the severity of her expression suggested that she might indeed hold it against you at a later time. She was very fond of Paschal, and got on better with him than with her mother. He was playful with her, and she liked that.

So back to the Monday, and what happened that day. Marianne was off work, Sheila was at school. Marianne decided to go to a hairdresser for a trim. She walked into a hairdressers in Grafton Street, having carefully unplaited her hair in a loo beforehand. Mondays are quiet, so she didn't need an appointment, and Aideen, the stylist to whom she was assigned, had plenty of time to deal with her. Aideen's eyes lit up with glee when she saw the magnificent tresses of beautifully conditioned healthy hair. Before she knew where she was, Marianne, normally a very strongminded person who knows exactly what she wants, was talked into having a major job done on her hair. Afterwards, she couldn't tell whether it was the sparkling enthusiasm of the stylist, or the fact that she wanted a change, but the upshot of it was that she remained in the hairdressers for three hours. Aideen, frustrated by miserable skimpy heads of hair, by head after head of boyish haircuts, was ecstatic. She was of the opinion that Lady Di had ruined women's hair forever and she went to town on Marianne. They chatted a lot, and Marianne,

169

despite herself, told Aideen a lot about her life. This was all very unlike her. It was as if a spell had been cast over her when she walked in the door of the salon. Some kind of magic spell that was mixed up in the bottles of lotions that added a chemically smell to the air. She spent an hour getting her hair washed, another hour getting it coloured with blonde streaks, and another hour getting a perm put in. Aideen wouldn't normally subject a head of hair to so much treatment on the one visit, but Marianne's hair was exceptionally sturdy. She was stunned by it and wanted her to come back to her night classes some time, so that she could sculpt Marianne's hair into the curves of a swan. Finally, Aideen blow-dried the hair into the most extraordinary shape, with playful curls and wispy runaway bits, and eventually Marianne found herself on the street, clasping the stylist's business card, feeling decidedly odd. While she was with Aideen, she found herself carried away by Aideen's enthusiasm, but on her own she felt a little foolish, a little unlike herself.

She went home and looked at herself in the mirror. She became obsessed with her hair and kept patting it and watching it spring back to its new artificial shape. She took off her plain navy gaberdine pinafore dress and put on a floral smock. A smock she normally didn't like, but somehow it suited the curls. She did a bit of spring cleaning around the house. She changed the sheets on the beds. On the linen shelf of the hot press, she found a duvet cover she had forgotten about. It was a wedding present she'd received eleven years ago and never used. It was from her lovely long-gone maiden aunt Carol, a satin peach affair, trimmed with a sumptuous amount of lace, and little satin bows. Not knowing quite why she was doing it, she swapped it for the blue and white striped one they normally used. The frilly duvet cover, which she had considered far too fluffy before, now seemed comforting in its frivolity. It was the kind of thing she would have loved when she was a teenager.

Sheila came home and stared at her mother for a while, and then burst into tears. She couldn't explain what was the matter. It wasn't that she didn't like the hair, it was just that everything seemed to have changed. The iron plait had symbolised normality for her. Her childish senses picked up the fact that something in Marianne's infrastructure had altered.

Paschal came home, and he was profoundly shocked. It wasn't just the hair, it was as if the hairdo had permeated the whole flat. Marianne, who normally strode purposefully around, now glided langorously. She normally looked at him openly, straightforwardly, but now she simpered at him, inclining her head oddly. She had ceased to be a woman, and had become a girl. He went to give her the customary peck on the cheek, and was repulsed by the salon smell. She smelt like his wife. Aargh!

For the rest of the evening, he stared at her oddly. Each time he turned towards her, he got a start. It was as if, suddenly, he was living with a stranger. When he went into the bedroom, and saw the bed, it was a total shock to him. That night, he couldn't sleep. Lace from the bedcover and pillows, the curls from Marianne's head kept tickling his nose.

The next day at work, her students all behaved differently to her. They smiled at her. One of them told her a joke. It seemed that she had lost all authority. She didn't seem to know how to behave with this haircut. She suspected one of the other tutors of giving her the eye. The director of the school stared in amazement at her.

Marianne was tremendously confused. She, who had an analytical mind, and prided herself on her self knowledge, simply didn't know how to assess the emotions she felt. Paschal got used to the new hair, and started to call her Mopsy, but Marianne didn't feel right. It wasn't that she wanted her old hair back, it was that she wanted a new spirit to go with the new hair. She could no longer cope. She couldn't get out of bed in the morning. She couldn't manage Sheila any longer. The iron in her psyche had melted.

For many many weeks, Paschal and Sheila visited her in the hospital. Here she wore a band around her hair, but wisps kept escaping, kept popping up like indomitable springs from a bust old armchair. She twittered like a bird, her eyes drifting in and out of focus. She had retreated within herself, gone to live in a private land. Paschal and Sheila despaired of ever having her back. But one day, when he went to visit her alone, she took off her headscarf, to rearrange it, and he could see that the curls were growing out. At the top of her head, at the roots, great strands of firm straw hairs were growing. The new hair was pushing away those wispy curls, pushing them away from her brain. Her eyes were still oddly vacant, but had a certain spark. He knew that she would heal herself. Not rapidly, but slowly and steadily.

"Will you bring me back a gift," he said, "from this place where you are now?"

"This is the land of the crumbled people," she said. "There are no gift shops here."

Opening Nights

The curtain came down on the final preview, and Jean nearly wept with relief. It was fine. She knew it was fine. All the performances, without exception, had arrived just where she wanted them. It had been a joy to watch the show. This was what it was all about, this feeling, this high. Jean gave some notes to the crew, and went backstage to give a last few words to the cast. They were all set for tomorrow's opening night. Jean let out a loud whoop and bellowed "Pub". Everybody heaved a sigh of relief. The director was happy. This was important. If the director was happy, they were all happy. They had to trust her to tell them that the show was OK.

When they got to the pub, Jean knocked back a couple of drinks very fast and talked incessantly, something that was unusual for her – normally she was subdued and observant in company. Marian Stewart, the lead actor, gave her a tight little hug and a kiss. She sensed Jean's cheer. They had worked together many times, their careers spanned twenty years, and they had built up a strong bond which frequently erupted into the bitter rows of close friendship, but was always fundamentally sound.

"Why do you do it?" Jean asked.

"Do what?"

"Act."

"Because I want to be famous. I know I may be taking my time, but I will get there. I plan to be a wonderful character actress any day now!" said Marian cheerfully.

Jean was dissatisfied with this answer.

"No," she said. "You act, you get up on that stage in front of all those people, because you want love."

"But I have lots of love. I'm very happy with Joseph. I have two lovely kids. I don't need love."

"You do. Us types . . ." and she pointed a slightly blurred finger from herself to Marian and back again. ". . . we need it. Ordinary love isn't good enough for us types. We are love-greedy. You act for applause. For that bit at the end where everybody claps you and everybody loves you. It's pathetic," she added cheerfully.

"Na. The applause isn't the best bit at all, Jean. It's nice, but it's not half as good as the unexpected gasps."

"Oh yeah, I'd forgotten about them."

Marian loved Jean and her funny notions. She was also quite used to Jean's habit of crashlanding just before opening nights.

Later on Maeve Witcher, the producer, came

into the pub to make sure that everybody was all right. She could see that Jean had settled in for the night. Maeve knew that it was a terrible thing to say and she would never say it out loud, but what Jean needed was a man. Maeve could see that independence was all very well. But really, what Jean needed was a nice man who would act as a carrot to get her home. It would steady her up. But there were problems with Jean. She could pick up the men all right, there was no doubt about that, she did it often enough, though these days it was getting a little less frequent. But she didn't seem to have the staying power, the follow-through, the attention to detail, the ability to make breakfast which is necessary to keep a man longer than the morning. In Maeve's view, what Jean really needed was a wife. Maeve could see that Jean was well on the way to being pissed. She sidled up to her at the bar. Jean turned to her and gave her a little drunken hug.

"Tell me, Maeve. I'm trying to figure this thing out. Why do you do it?"

"Do what?"

"Do this creative work."

"Oh, so my work is 'creative' now, is it? I thought I was a 'dilettante who could only tell my arse from my elbow because there was more fat on my arse.'"

Maeve had never forgiven Jean for that one. It had been a product of an argument they had had a couple of months back.

"Don't mind me. I talk shite." Jean never took

her arguments with anybody very seriously. She didn't realise how insulting and harsh she could be. Always ready to forgive, she expected always to be forgiven.

Maeve considered the question for a moment, then answered:

"I suppose I do it because I'm good at it."

Jean thought about the way that Maeve flitted about at launches and receptions, shoving canapés or whatever the fuck they were called under people's noses, pouring wine, coaxing everybody into a good mood. Jean thought about the utter charm with which Maeve dealt with financiers, and the lovely gentle smile that looked almost real, which broke across her face as investors fell for her dulcet deals. Jean thought about the wretchedness experienced by Maeve when a deal fell through.

"No. You do this because you want love."

Maeve looked puzzled, and then shrugged her shoulders. Jean always went a bit odd when a play opened. A bit philosophical. Maeve called it her post-natal period.

The pub started to thin out. One by one the company left. Maeve was determined to stay in the pub until Jean left, so she could prevent her from deciding to do anything wild. She needed her in the morning. Jean was wise to her, though, and got into a private director-actor discussion in the corner with Rebecca, the youngest member of the cast, forcing Maeve to either sit on her own or leave. Maeve knew she was defeated, and saw no option but to buzz off home. She reminded Jean of her duties the following day, having lunch with the writer and so on. "I'll phone you in the morning as soon as I know what time he's getting in, and we'll set up lunch. Provisionally, one o'clock in Jaspers, OK?"

"Sure darling, give me a bell." Jean smiled and waved triumphantly at her. She loved winning Maeve's games. She turned back to her conversation with Rebecca. Jean was never very comfortable with Rebecca. Rebecca did the only nude scene in the play, and Jean knew she was very unhappy doing it, though she never directly said so. Her youth made her obsessive about her professionalism. Jean felt bad about this, but she didn't let herself get too worked up about it. There were other things she felt bad and worse about.

"Why do you do it, Rebecca?"

"Do the nude scene?"

"No. I mean act."

"Oh." Rebecca blushed.

"I suppose 'cos I love being on the stage. I'm at my happiest while I'm on the stage."

"But why?"

"Well, I suppose I like pretending to be somebody other than myself."

Rebecca pulled on her coat and made her escape calling "See ya tomorrow. Don't forget your beauty sleep."

"Bye darling."

As Jean watched Rebecca's mop of hair exit, she thought that, above all, Rebecca did it because she wanted love. She wanted it desperately.

A little bit of Jean died that day in rehearsal when she made Rebecca take her clothes off. Rebecca was young, eighteen, this was her first big break. It was her first real chance. She had been reared with a code of strict modesty. Jean had told her at the audition that the character would have to do a nude scene, and Rebecca had accepted that. But when the time came, she froze. Jean had been patient and said that they'd leave it for that day. And they left it for another day. But as time went on, and opening night got closer, Jean's patience ebbed away, and she told Rebecca to get her clothes off now, or not to bother coming back after lunch. Rebecca, almost teary, did so. She took off her clothes article by article and dropped them in a heap on the floor. She then stood naked in the centre of the room, bright red from her forehead to her shoulders, crucified with shame. Her shame made all the others in the room turn away. Jean stared on defiantly. She stared at Rebecca's body. It was truly beautiful. Slight and soft as only an eighteen-year-old body can be. Rebecca kept her gaze firmly on the floor. Mortified. She shifted from foot to foot. Jean went on with the rehearsal and wouldn't let Rebecca put her clothes back on. She made her work naked for two hours. She hated what this girl's upbringing had done to her. This bloody country. All bitterly tangled up in some ludicrous notion of modesty, full of denial of its bodily functions. A country that paid lipservice to motherhood and denied the sexual activity necessary to achieve the state. Irish morality seemed to be embodied at its most pathetic in Rebecca. At the end of the session, she let everybody else go and kept Rebecca for a moment. She explained to her that she should love her body. That it was a thing of beauty. That it should never be a source of shame. Rebecca put her clothes on and agreed. She agreed with her voice, but Jean could tell by her eyes, those lost eyes, that she would never forgive her. From then on, there had never been a murmur from Rebecca when it came to that scene.

Jean was alone in the pub. She didn't want to go home, but couldn't think where else to go. She felt great, happy, full, it would have been a shame to go home and waste the good mood. Good moods weren't two a penny anymore. Maybe she should have hung on to Maeve, but Maeve always went home early. Maeve always went home to Mark, or Morkyboots, or whatever she called her dreary husband. Maeve was a dead loss for the crack. The barmen were bellowing that they wanted the pub cleared, so Jean staggered to her feet and out onto the street. The streets were full. It was the night of the Leaving Cert results. Teenagers seemed to be getting younger and better-looking every year. They also looked happier. She wasn't so happy looking when she was that age. She was sure of it. She decided to go for a pizza.

She went to a restaurant she'd never been to before, because she didn't want to meet anyone that she knew. She sat in the corner and took out her two favourite reviews whch she always kept in a notebook in her handbag. She carried them with her everywhere in case she had an ego emergency. They were rave reviews. One from her earliest days – "Most promising newcomer . . ." Another from a later date – "Jean Fox proves herself to be among the finest directors around." There had been other reviews, bad ones, but Jean happily threw them away. She only kept the good ones. She ordered a pizza with pepperoni and chillies. Extra chillies – she fancied some intense sensation, and chose a dry white wine from the list. A full bottle. Some of the people in the restaurant looked at her oddly. Jean eyeballed them back. Solitary dining at midnight was a social crime for a woman. Her presence seemed to have upset an entire table seated under a palm tree opposite, who could hardly manage to eat their food. They were a bit drunk and didn't seem to realise their voices carried.

"Maybe she's been stood up," said the boy in the white runners who could barely speak. His girlfriend, or at least the woman who was fondling his inner thigh, thought that it was really sad for a woman of forty or thereabouts to be dining on her own at that hour. She hoped that it wouldn't happen to her, and she looked at the tennis-shoed boy plaintively, and kissed him. She aimed for his mouth, but got him on the nose. After a little more talk amongst themselves, one of the group staggered over to Jean.

"Hi! We just thought that you were lonely, and we thought that maybe you'd like to join us. We're not great company, in fact we're probably not even good company, but we're better than nobody." Jean's first instinct was to say no. This crowd seemed insipid, bordering on the objectionable. But she was a little bit taken with the humility of the boy who offered the invitation, and she was bored. They were all in their early twenties, and obviously couldn't hold their drink. Jean joined them, and brought her bottle of wine over, which she poured out. It would have been too much for her anyway. They all worked in a restaurant together, and this was half the staff, the other half was working. But they'd be finished at two, and then there was a party in Biff's Gaff. Did she want to come?

Jean strolled with them to Biff's Gaff, which, despite its grandiose title, turned out to be a minute bedsit on the South Circular Road. Twenty people piled in, and somebody rolled a joint. Jean began to unwind and enjoy herself. A bottle of Tequila was produced from someone's inside pocket, nicked earlier from The Stag's Head. It all reminded Jean of her own early twenties. This was exactly what they used to do. She had thought that it would go on forever, but the inevitable happened. One by one they had fallen in love. Some of them were happy. Jean had launched a divorce campaign, but then the kids started to arrive. Jean's friends had a talent for marriage. This crowd seemed to be very nice. Very friendly. Not the slightest bit intrigued at her presence there. Biff was a bit of a comedian, and kept them all entertained for about an hour singlehandedly. The gathering began to thin out. People went home or crashed out. Jean didn't feel tired. She didn't want to go home. She loved the night and wanted it to go on forever. Finally just herself and Biff were left, drinking tea. Biff was about twenty-two and very good-looking. He was smart and alert and funny, the kind of boy whom Jean might have fallen for twenty years earlier. He too loved the night. He flirted with her a little. And she enjoyed flirting back at him. She was old enough to be his mother, but she liked that. She wondered should she invite him back to her place. Suddenly she got the sensation that she was doing all the talking. Biff excused himself and went to the loo and never came back. Jean left.

She hailed a cab on the street outside. It was six o'clock, and a lovely warm morning. Jean felt young again. Her body felt light and airy. When the taxi let her off at her Ballsbridge apartment, she did a little dance in the morning air. Once inside she attempted to do some simple household tasks. She tried to empty the dishwasher and put away the delph, but it all proved too much for her. She put down some milk for her cat, Minnie, who gave her a wide berth. She spilt milk on the floor. Minnie sidled cautiously over to it, but Jean ambushed her on the way and gave her a massive cuddle. The cat endured the cuddle and, as soon as she could escape from Jean, went for the milk. "Cold bitch," Jean muttered, as she went blearily to bed.

Tomorrow, tomorrow, tomorrow came. Jean lay

awake in bed listening to the furious Maeve leave messages on her answering machine. Jean knew she should get up and get dressed to meet Jeremy Wright, the writer. Wright the writer. Mr Wright. Instead, she lay in bed and stared at the ceiling. Hours passed. She stared, and resolved never to get up. Finally, in the early afternoon, Minnie came into the room and sat on her head, demanding dinner. Jean burrowed her head under the pillow and the cat trotted down her body and dug her claws into her stomach. Jean eventually hauled herself out of bed and threw some muesli in a bowl. She then played back the four irate messages from Maeve.

She played them a second time. They were great messages. The first one was kind of chirpy and good morning-ish. Jean remembered the time, twenty years before, when they had shared a flat on Pembroke Road, that she had taught Maeve how to wake her up in the morning. Maeve had come into her room one morning and barked at her to get the hell up out of bed. Jean had emerged downstairs about five minutes later choking with sobs, and totally wild.

"Don't you ever wake me up like that ever again. I cannot stand people giving out to me in the morning. Don't you ever ever do that to me again."

Maeve had been quite shocked, Jean was normally so calm and good-humoured. But Jean wasn't quite herself for a while in the morning. It took her some time to adjust to the day. There were fifteen minutes at the start of the day, just before the first cup of tea, when it was decidedly touch-and-go. She was better at night.

Twenty years later, Maeve hadn't forgotten. It was a gentle message. The second was gentle enough too. By the third, you could hear the patience had totally gone, though the tone was still upbeat. The fourth one sounded positively injured. Jean played them one more time. It was amazing how comfortable Maeve sounded on the answering machine. She sounded so controlled. The phone went again, and Jean let the machine answer it. It was Maeve again, this time with an angry edge to her voice. "Jean, I met him for lunch, and he's grand. You're a disaster. I'll kill you. See you at the theatre."

Jean knew that Maeve knew that she was listening to the message. Jean remembered when she and Maeve used to be real friends, not the pretend ones they were now, each obviously out of patience with the other, but too old or too busy to take issue. Neither bothered to fight for the remnants of their friendship. They became used to its decay, as one did to slowly staining wallpaper.

In the late afternoon, Jean went into the theatre to attend to some final bits and pieces. Maeve was there, fussing with the front of house staff and getting press packages together. Jean kept dodging her. She knew she should apologise about the missed lunch, but wanted to do it later, when she felt calmer. Maeve fired the odd fierce look across the room at her, and Jean pretended not to notice.

At seven o'clock, Jean took a taxi home to get changed into her glad rags.

Jean went to her wardrobe and pulled out the usual opening night finery. She threw on the clothes and slapped some brown muck on her face, a streak of pink lipstick and some purple eyeshadow. There was nothing subtle about Jean's opening night face. Minnie the cat stared at her calmly. Again, Jean ambushed her for a cuddle. "Minnie cat, wish me good luck for tonight." Minnie stared at her, unmoved. Jean thought that the cat was becoming increasingly hostile to her.

Meanwhile, at the theatre, Maeve Witcher allowed herself half a glass of wine and chatted to the people around. All the critics and important guests had arrived and Maeve had introduced everybody to everybody. When the show came down there would be a reception with wine and canapés for the guests. Maeve felt satisfied with herself. She knew she was a brilliant producer. Everything she did got maximum coverage and, if the shows themselves didn't always do well, it certainly wasn't her fault.

Jean wasn't back yet, and Maeve hoped that she'd make it. The problem with Jean was that she was unpredictable. Talented, but not totally reliable. Jean burst in the door in layers and layers of ill-matched finery and dripping with cheap but ornate costume jewellery. Maeve occupied herself with her notes. She was in a rage, but didn't want to show it at this moment. A row with Jean would not be appropriate at two minutes to eight on opening night. Jean was in quite a flap. The curtain was just about to go up. She was delighted that she didn't have time to talk to Maeve who was sitting on a foyer barstool looking at some notes. Probably estimating profits, or looking for a penny in her books. She was always complaining about missing pennies. Jean slipped quietly into the auditorium and took a seat at the very back.

She watched the audience respond to her work. She monitored the predicted responses and the unpredicted ones. The laughs in places she didn't expect. The performances rising to the full and enthusiastic house. The interval arrived and Jean mingled with the first night crowd. The general response to the play seemed favourable. Jean was careful to keep herself at the opposite side of the foyer from Maeve. Despite all her efforts, Maeve cornered her. Jean steeled herself for an onslaught, but there was no need. Maeve had her opening night face on and beamed at her.

"Jean, are you OK? You look a bit tired. Did you get my messages? C'mere, let me introduce you to Jeremy Wright. He's lovely, very relaxed."

Jean allowed herself to be led off like a lamb.

Mr Jeremy Wright was at the bar smiling and being nice to everyone. Jean grabbed a glass of wine on the way over to him. His handshake was warm and firm and he had one of those faces that remind you of a friendly dog. Around the forty mark, Jean guessed. Her knees began to shake as she stood there and said nothing.

"Well?" she demanded.

"Well what?"

"What do you think of it?"

"Oh I'm so sorry. I've been raving about it to everybody so far I forgot to rave about it to you. I love it. It's great. Better than the London production. It really suits the Irish voice."

Jean's knees stopped shaking at this and they settled into a friendly discussion about the play. Maeve observed that things were going smoothly, and left them to it. She forayed off into the throng once more to butter up a press person, before going off for a sneak preview nibble of the tasty canapés. Maeve had toned down the refreshments for this production, because the last time she'd hired such an exotic caterer, the canapés upstaged the show. Maeve did one more check that Jean was not alienating the nice Englishman, before everyone filed back into the auditorium.

The second half of the show went as well as the first. Jean sat with the writer. He seemed very nice. He also seemed thrilled with the production. Jean was glad. It would have been a major stress if he had been difficult.

After the show, the invited guests stayed back for Maeve's reception. This was the bit that Jean loathed, these awful affairs where Jean had to talk to people. She arrived and immediately grabbed a glass of wine. Maeve came over to her and gave Jean and the glass a meaningful look. Maeve worried about how unreliable Jean could be when she was drinking. Jean boldly continued to drink the wine. Maeve gave a short little breath.

The actors were all scattered about, chatting and glowing from the first night. Lots of people came up to Jean and congratulated her on the show, telling her how wonderful it was. Jean didn't believe them. They were all lying. It was a major conspiracy. Jeremy Wright was lying too. Rebecca came over to Maeve and thanked her. She too was lying. Jean knew that Rebecca was lying, that she hated doing the show, that her part was stupid. Jean wished that she had the guts to have it out with Rebecca, but she smiled vacantly as the vulnerable mop of hair bobbed back into the revelling crowd.

Maeve Witcher flitted about and chatted to everybody. It seemed to come easily to her. Jean stood frozen in a corner. She was, as usual, overcome with a terrible shyness. She wanted to talk to people but simply couldn't. It was odd. She was the most confident person in the world in a rehearsal room, or in any professional capacity, formidable even. But leave her without a minder in a public relations situation, and she dried up completely. The show was up. Jean no longer had a function. She had nothing to get out of bed for. There was no point to her. She took another glass of wine.

Jean thought about her next project. It wasn't until the middle of Autumn. The time between now and then stretched ahead like a huge icy ocean, full of Minnie's alienating stares. She looked around the room. Everybody seemed happy. They seemed to be having a great time. Were they pretending? They suddenly seemed ridiculous to her. Maeve's tinny hollow laugh. The actors with their hyper-energy. The first nighters in their funny clothes. Jeremy Wright turned up at her side.

"I see you're not that comfortable at these things."

"No. How did you guess?"

He smiled at her with his friendly eyes.

"I've never been to Dublin before. Can you believe it? So, I think I'm going to hang around for a few days. Maybe, if you're not too busy, you could be a bit of a guide for me, make up for standing me up today."

"I'm terribly sorry, it's just . . ."

"No need to apologise. I know better than anybody how hectic opening nights can be."

Maeve arrived over and whisked Jeremy off to be introduced to Marian Stewart. Jean sighed. Maeve was always doing that. Her timing was abysmal. Jean took another glass of wine and looked around. She could see young Rebecca over in the far corner being chatted up by an older actor, a very talented guy, and a bit of a lecher. He had featured in Jean's lurid past. Poor Rebecca. No guts, just wandering around life being a victim of other people's designs. But she was young, and that was a great advantage. In time, she'd learn how not to be a fool.

Maeve had rescued Jeremy from Jean, who was very nearly pissed. Now. Who else needed attention? She could see that Rebecca was being chatted up by whatshisname who was a total tart. He had been fucked by the entire city. Well, that was Rebecca's problem. Maeve could not be expected to chaperone everybody.

Jeremy congratulated Marian on her performance. He loved her in the part. In fact he loved everything and everybody. Marian had to ask Jeremy what he was trying to do with her character's monologue in Act 2. She had never quite cracked it, never quite been happy with it. There was always one piece in a performance that didn't quite sit right. There was always something unachieved. Jeremy explained in gentle tones what he had meant with the speech. Marian's character was a development of an idea that he had had in his first play.

"I started writing quite by accident. I was working in sales and wrote a play to keep myself amused on the train journey into work. Commuter trains are quite inspiring. It was an instant hit. A comedy, *Life of a Salesman*. Maybe you've heard of it? I haven't looked back since."

"Jean says people write because they need love."

"Maybe they do. I write because I need money," he quipped.

Marian burst out laughing.

Maeve was chatting amiably to somebody from a gossip column when she sensed a sudden change of atmosphere in the room. She was sensitive to atmosphere changes in rooms. Everybody was looking over at the corner of the bar. Maeve excused herself and manoeuvred herself into a position with a good view.

Jean was causing the commotion. She was sitting on a barstool with no clothes on. Her garments lay in a heap on the floor beside her. She still had on her jewellery. Her forty-three-year old flesh had aged well. Maeve was appalled. She had just been thinking how well the whole thing was going. Jean hadn't looked that pissed. Maeve made a beeline for her. Jeremy got there first.

Jeremy laughed with his eyes.

"Jean. What are you doing?"

"I'm showing solidarity with the actress who has to take off her clothes," she whispered into his ear with a giggle.

Jeremy laughed out loud. He was too embarrassed to look at her body, so he just held her eye instead. Jean could see consternation on Maeve's face over his shoulder, but she didn't care.

"So you will show me around. That's great. I can imagine the town would be a bit of a laugh with you as my guide."

A smile spread across Jean's face and she started to laugh quietly. She could see Maeve's expression soften, she too developed a grin. Maeve did have a mad streak in her but she didn't nourish it often. You would almost forget that behind the current Maeve there lurked a carefree dervish who had, one summer night, dived naked into the Liffey and swum across it just for "Fun". A huge thunderclap of laughter escaped from Maeve, a massive belly-ache of laughter. Jean joined her with a quieter laugh, one that shook her shoulders and her flesh. The two women's eyes met, and Jean remembered why it was that they had become such good friends. Their twinkling eyes held for a moment, before Maeve broke away.

Jean turned her attention back to Jeremy.

"Why do you do it?" she asked him.

"Do what?"

"Write."

"Oh that's easy. Because I need love," he said.

Maeve went to the other side of the room and steered the gossip columnist from the *Independent* over to a position where she had a good view of Jean. It would make brilliant copy, and the *Independent*'s photographer was still here. You couldn't buy publicity like that.

"That's it," squealed Jean. "That's exactly it. We do it because we need love."

Suddenly the next few days of her life seemed to have a lot more potential than they had a glass of wine ago. Jeremy was still too embarrassed to look at her body and was staring straight into her eyes. "What are you thinking?" she asked.

"Your eyes. They're the colour of the sky on a day when the sun doesn't know whether to stay in or come out."

"A poet," she thought.

"You are very charming, Mr Wright," and she brightened. Her heart lifted.